WHAT READERS ARE SAYING ABOUT
THE TRUE LIES OF REMBRANDT STONE:

So, I read this book in one sitting. ONE. I never do that, ever. Seriously, ever. It's that good. Between life responsibilities and my short attention span, it simply never happens. Oh, but Rembrandt Stone and Eve. What a ride! This series is shaping up to be my favorite so far this year and we're only two books into a six book series. The plot twists and turns kept me guessing and muttering 'no, no, noooooo' more than once, but the characters are what I love best.

Rembrandt for all his flaws and regrets is the kind of guy you can't help but love and want to see get things right. He and Eve's life together has been rife with complication, pain at times, but so worth it. The continued peel-back of their history together kept me turning pages with gusto.

Kelly, Goodreads

Oh my word! Where do I even begin? Love suspense? Read this book. Love time travel? Read this book. Love to have the unexpected happen? Read this book. Love going through the ups and downs with the characters? You know what I'm going to say, right?

I like to take my time reading stories. Take them at a decent pace. Not possible with Rem's story. I had no choice but to swipe furiously through it because I HAD to know what was going to happen! I felt like every page held a piece of Rembrandt's disintegrating reality. I didn't expect to finish it in a day. The writing was just so good. It hooked me, reeled me in, and didn't release me until... well, I was going to say the last page, but that only propelled me into book three because I wasn't released! Gah! So good!

Mimi, Goodreads

The True Lies
of Rembrandt Stone

Cast the First Stone

No Unturned Stone

Sticks and Stone

Set in Stone

Blood from a Stone

Heart of Stone

No Unturned Stone

TRISTONE

TriStone Media Group
Minneapolis, MN

Tristone Media Inc.

15100 Mckenzie Blvd

Minnetonka, Minnesota, 55345

Copyright © 2021 by Tristone Media

ISBN: 978-1-954023-03-1

www.RembrandtStone.com

SOLI DEO GLORIA

CHAPTER 1

Just try and outrun your demons, I dare you.

I sit in my daughter's upstairs bedroom, in my half-remodeled craftsman, the morning bright against the window, holding a black teddy bear in my shaking hands. Gomer, a throwaway gift to my then four-year-old daughter, almost an afterthought I picked up from a drugstore as I raced home from work on a long-ago birthday.

A white star is embedded in the toy's fur, and this version of Gomer still has both eyes. They stare at me, black, glassy.

Shocked.

It's all wrong.

Please, God, let me wake up.

It's a fear that stalks every man, at least the ones like me, middle-aged, married, a father of one, trying to frame his life into something that resembles success. A fear that, despite his heroic attempts, and as much as he tries to live in the light, his mistakes will find him.

And the price of those mistakes will cost him everything.

The voice that confirms it is seven years old, a deafening

memory deep inside my head. "But daddy, you're a detective. You know how to find things."

Overnight my life has imploded.

My house is now a war zone, the product of fury and panic, the drawers opened, dumped out, my office bearing the wreckage of my disbelief. I spent the past hour digging through my belongings—our belongings—to find anything that might give me answers.

My seven-year-old daughter, Ashley, has vanished. No, that's not accurate. She's been murdered. Two years ago.

My beautiful wife, Eve, has left me. She wants a divorce from the man I've become.

A man I don't know.

And I haven't a clue how to get them back.

But I've jumped too far ahead. Ironically, I'll have to rewind time, return to the moment when the demons knocked on my door in the form of my ex-partner, a box of cold cases and a gift— an old watch bequeathed by my boss, Chief of Police, John Booker.

No, maybe I'll start later that night, when, after shaking awake from a nightmare, I stumbled downstairs to my office, the one with the less-than-inspirational leather chair my wife gave me when I left the force three years ago, and began to work on my unfinished novel.

Eve found me in the middle of the night as I sat there, barely dressed, trying to find words to add to my unfinished manuscript. She dragged out the cold cases and pulled the first one, the coffee-shop bombings of 1997, the one where we first met.

The catalyst for this entire nightmare.

That's when I put on the watch.

I couldn't believe Booker left me his prized possession. I don't remember a day he didn't wear it. An old watch with a worn leather wristband and a face like a vintage clock, the gears visible through the glass.

The hands didn't move, stuck on the five and the three, even when I wound it. On the back two words etched into the steel: Be Stalwart.

I hope so, because this morning, when I realized what the watch had cost me, I threw it against the wall, snatched it off the floor and threw it again when it refused to work.

And you might think, calm down, Rembrandt, just get another watch.

But it's this watch that has somehow loosed the demons.

And I must find a way to send them back.

Now, as I sit in the wreckage of my life, I wiggle the dial again, shaking the watch, pressing it to my head. Please, please—

I don't really know what I'm asking for, because the truth is, well, unbelievable.

I dreamed—or did?—travel back in time. Solved the coffee shop bombing case. Then I woke up and everything...everything...

Oh, God—

"Rem?" A knock sounds on my open door—I didn't close it after Eve left, just an hour ago after handing me divorce papers. I remember dropping the packet on my rush up the stairs to Ashley's room to confirm Eve's wretched words.

"Ashley was murdered, remember? Two years ago."

I don't remember much after that.

"Rembrandt?" The voice makes me look up and probably it's a good thing the law just walked into the room because this is a crime scene.

My life has been stolen.

"Burke," I say, and I'm not even a little embarrassed that I've been crying. That my house looks vandalized. That I want to shake him for answers.

Andrew Burke was my partner for the better part of twenty years. A tall, bald, dark-skinned detective of the Minneapolis Police department, he's my best friend and sparring partner, even now.

Answers. He'll help me find them—

"Don't tell me you're on a bender again."

What?

Burke is wearing a suit, of course. I ditched mine after a few years on the job, but he always looked good in them. I was more of a sweater and jeans guy, and back then, I wore my hair long, with a hint of a beard, Don Johnson style. It was a thing. And Eve liked it.

Eve. The scene flashes through my mind again—Eve on the doorstep with her assistant, Silas. Eve handing me a manila envelope, Silas's arm around her. My insane urge to sink my fist into his mouth. Then the words—oh, God, the words—She's dead, Rem. She's dead, and you can't bring her back.

"No, I—" I stare again at Gomer, still in my grip.

"Aw, shoot," Burke says, his tone softening. "Eve told me you weren't doing well."

"Eve told you…"

"You fought again didn't you?"

My mouth opens and his words find the air around me, but don't land. Eve and I don't fight. At least, not about anything important. Sure, the occasional missed pickup at school, and she hates when I leave my socks on the stairs, but—

"I told her to wait and give you the divorce papers at work. I know yesterday was a hard day for you." He sighs, and I look back up at him. "I'm sorry man, but you knew this was coming."

I knew…

I can't breathe, my chest actually constricting, and I press my hand to it. Because twenty-four hours ago my wife was in my warm bed, my daughter in the next room surrounded by freshly unwrapped birthday gifts and my biggest trial was suffering from writer's block.

Then I had a dream—

No, then I…

I put my head between my knees.

"Rem! Sheesh, breathe." Burke leans down in front of me, his hand on my shoulder. "C'mon, don't do this to me again."

Again? But at least Burke is still my best friend, still the guy who won't let me drown.

"Dude. Listen, I get it. You're not the only one who wanted to forget yesterday's anniversary. But, it's been two years. Two." He draws a long breath. "It's time to at least try to move on."

I stare at him. "Ashley's dead." I am just trying out the words because, you know, she's not dead, not in my, um, timeline, my real timeline, but here— maybe here is all I have—

Now I can't breathe again.

"Yes," Burke says. "Yes she is." He sighs, and concern fills his dark eyes.

"How, when?" Because maybe if I have answers—

"No, Rem. We're not doing this again. You've read the file a thousand times."

The file. The file. In the box of files Booker gave me, all cold cases from my time on the job.

Maybe it's still here, sitting on the floor by the chair where Eve left it last night.

I toss Gomer aside, scramble past him, down the stairs and into my office.

I kneel beside the box, stacked high with folders, and rifle through them.

I stop, a coldness surging through me. It's gone. The file from the bombing case, the one I went back to solve—and yes, that still sounds crazy to me—

It's gone.

But of course it is. Because I, you know, solved it.

So it's not there. It can't be. But …

"What are you doing?" Burke says as he comes in and crouches again beside me.

"I'm just looking—" I see the cases I know too well. The working girl found near one of my favorite bars. A nurse, found in a parking lot in the middle of January. A waitress outside an uptown diner, and the worst—yes, it's still here.

I pull it out and groan.

The death of Eve's father, Minneapolis Deputy Police Inspector Danny Mulligan, and her kid brother, Asher. Skinny kid, smart, a hacker.

Asher saw me kiss Eve, and for a second the taste of her is on my lips. I kissed her last night, in her house, the smell of sawdust and summer in the air.

Real. The dream felt, smelled, and tasted real.

"It's not here." I set down Danny and Asher's file and keep looking, just to confirm.

"What's not there?"

"Ashley—where's her file?"

Burke is looking at me and now he shakes his head. "Get your head on and get down to the precinct. The Jackson murders aren't going to solve themselves." He turns away, runs his hand over his smooth head.

Last time I saw him, he had hair. That thought slides into my brain, and yes, maybe I'm having a nervous breakdown, a split with reality. He looks at me. "I know you're hurting, Rem, but you're freakin' me out."

Yeah, well, I'm freaking myself out too. But, "Where is Ashley's file?"

"C'mon, Rem."

"Tell me!"

"It's where it's been for the last two years! With all the other Jackson murders."

Who's Jackson? But I don't ask, because Burke is wearing a thin look. "Listen, I can't afford to have the head of the task force laying on his bathroom floor, drunk."

Again, drunk? Although, my gaze goes to my empty glass on the desk. One lousy shot of Macallans and suddenly I'm drunk?

Burke looks a little desperate now and it's an uncommon expression that unnerves me, too. "We finally caught a break—a survivor—and we need you on your game for this afternoon's press conference. We're close, Rem, you told me that yourself."

I did? But I nod. What I really want to do is bang my head on something, dislodge the memories that are stuck deep inside of a world I don't know, don't understand, but have clearly lived in.

He heads for the door. Pauses. "Come in, get to work. Please don't make me fire you."

Fire me? Burke is my boss?

I guess that feels right—I always knew he had leadership in him.

He leaves me there, and in a moment I hear his car drive away.

Work? Oh, I'm going to work all right.

To a job I remember quitting three years ago.

So the demons couldn't find me.

But apparently, I'll have to face those demons, if I want answers.

CHAPTER 2

In my line of work, I've met plenty of the mentally ill. People who claim to hear voices, who believe in altered realities, even a few whose illness has split them into different personalities. They become people they're not, who wouldn't recognize themselves.

For a moment, as I scan my kitchen, I wonder if I'm in that category. An empty bottle of Macallans—at least I'm consistent if not spendy—sits in my sink, along with an empty high-ball. In a Styrofoam container on the counter are the bones of wings from a takeout place down the street. (It does give me some small comfort that I'm still ordering from Gino's in this reality. Clearly, I haven't completely lost my mind.)

But maybe I have lost it, because in the recycling, which emits an odor that might raise the dead, I notice about four too many crushed beer cans.

On another bender, was what Burke said, and a look at my house tells me that I've had a rough couple of years. The dining room remodeling project is still unfinished, but now wires dangle from where the light fixture should hang from the ceiling, a pile of unfinished baseboards sit along the wall, and no paint yet on the sheet-rocked walls. A layer of dust films the sheet over the table.

I notice other things, also, as I dump the bag of recycling by the back door.

No swing set in the backyard. But the towering dead elm that used to loom over the house is gone so at least I got that far.

My wife's satchel is not hanging from her hook in the mudroom. Nor her car keys, with her C.S.I keychain: Can't Stand Idiots.

Agreed. I used to joke that I didn't know why she stayed with me, then.

The old laughter, so easy in the past, boils a hole through me now.

I walk through the family room—the picture of my girls on the beach at Eve's parents' home still hangs on the wall, a film of dust obscuring the pane. Ashley, age three, digging in the sand, wearing a bright pink swimsuit. Eve is sitting beside her, her face in shadow under a brimmed hat, grinning for me. The picture became my screen saver on my computer and Eve had it framed for me that next Christmas.

I'm going to retch.

I take the stairs two at a time, slide into the bathroom on my knees, but nothing rises. But a sweat has broken out across my forehead and I'm pitiful as I stand and look in the mirror.

Go to work.

Burke's voice in my head, thundering.

You're a detective, Daddy.

I clasp my hands over my face.

I took a shower earlier, right before my life imploded, but as I look in the mirror, I feel dirty, ancient, wearing a layer of dark whiskers, my eyes reddened, as if yes, I spent the night face down, clutching that bottle of single malt.

I've never had a drinking problem, although maybe I should have, given the disasters of my childhood. It's possible, however, the loss of Ashley in this timeline drove me to dark, previously off-limits places.

I shave, brush my teeth, wash my face. A couple eyedrops and I'm a close replica of the man I knew.

My closet is devoid of my wife's clothing. And clearly in this new life, I've forgotten how to do laundry.

This version of me isn't one I want to know.

I find a clean pair of jeans and a button down and realize I don't have my wallet. It's still in my jeans, hanging in the bathroom downstairs where I grabbed my morning shower.

The wallet I had when I, yes, went back to 1997.

That still sounds crazy, but given the proof...

I race downstairs and grab the jeans.

A fist forms in my gut as I empty the pockets, find my worn leather wallet and flip it open.

Everything inside me empties as I rifle through it.

It's gone. The picture I took with Ashley last year at the Mall of America. The shot had been of us on the log chute, a water ride. She's screaming, her eyes wide, blonde hair flying as she holds onto the bars, spray lifting around us. I'm grinning, my eyes on Ash, so much love in my expression I don't recognize myself.

Gone, now just a ghost in my memory.

No. This can't be right. Ashley is still out there.

I just need to find her.

I grab the recycling and head out into the garage and nearly weep at the sight of my 1988 Porsche, black and shiny, sitting the garage. I've had it since I bought it out of impound, and worked for hours under the hood to bring her back to life. I get in, the leather warm and familiar, and turn her over. She purrs under my hands.

Finally, someone I know. Someone familiar. A friend.

The station is set on a familiar KQ92, and as I pull out, I turn up the radio, just to drown out the thunder of my heartbeat.

I'm beating out Journey's Stone in Love on my steering wheel, trying to keep myself from punching it and committing a misdemeanor.

Stay calm. Nothing would be solved by taking out a mailbox on the way to the precinct.

Our neighborhood is surrounded by other vintage craftsman homes, with wide front porches, manicured lawns and the aura of lives lived well. A woman jogging with a stroller lifts her hand to me and I recognize her—Gia, from across the street.

My last memory of Gia was her flirting with Russell, the former Vikings linebacker who lives next door. In that version, Gia was recently separated from Alex, her husband. I wonder who the baby belongs to as I lift a hand back. Apparently, I'm a good neighbor in this version, too. I don't know why that's important to me, but the fist in my chest loosens a little.

The sky is bright, the air loose and filled with the scents of summer—freshly cut grass, lilacs still blooming along the street. I drive by the lake on the way to the precinct and for a moment, Eve is sitting beside me.

Her auburn hair is down, taken by the wind through the open window and she's grinning at me. Her shoes are off, a little paint on her toenails and she's wearing a blue sun dress. She looks over at me and grins.

I am undone.

I turn off the radio and drive the rest of the way in silence.

The precinct is as familiar as my old Chuck Taylors. Housed in an historic downtown building, made of rose granite, it has a city clock that rises nearly thirty stories above the street and gongs out the late hour of my arrival.

I pull into the lot behind the building and shake away the swift memory of me in my Camaro of yesteryear.

Yesterday.

In fact, it feels as if I was just here as I hoof it inside, past the massive rotunda with the giant King Neptune sprawled in the center. I rub his right toe for luck, then head toward the city police annex and follow the hall down to the conference room.

Twenty-four hours and twenty-plus years ago, I was staring at pictures of the coffee shop bombing victims.

Now, the conference room walls are a collage of names, photographs, timelines, and scene descriptions connected by notes and lines and my own chicken scratchings. I recognize Eve's name on a few of the reports, her signature above the line, Director, Department of Crime Scene Investigation.

I don't know why that brings a sigh of relief. At the very least, I know we have the best person on the job.

"You made it," Burke says, and I turn. He hands me a cup of coffee. "I would have thought you'd wear a suit for the press conference."

Press conference? Oh no.

"You can borrow one of my suit coats," he says, then approaches the board. "We got lucky this time. A survivor. Have you talked with her yet?"

There are over a dozen pictures on the wall, all of girls ages fifteen to thirty, and my body turns cold.

What is this?

I approach the board and scan my bad handwriting.

All the girls were strangled, their bodies found in lonely places—a park, an alleyway, a dumpster, an abandoned warehouse.

19

And with every body, a twenty dollar bill with the words thank you for your service, written in black ink.

Right. The Jackson murders. As in Andrew Jackson, from the twenty dollar calling card. I wonder if I coined the name because that feels like something out of the mind of a novelist.

Am I still a novelist?

My gaze falls on a picture. Not Ashley's—that might have had me gripping my knees, or on the floor, but of...no, please no... I swallow hard.

"John Booker is a victim of the Jackson killer?" His picture is tacked away from the others, and it's his official mug. He's in uniform, stars on his shoulder, wearing his badge, salt and pepper hair, keen eyes, his face solemn.

He can see into my soul, so I look away and take a sip of the coffee, hoping it's bracing.

Burke is frowning at me, so I ask, "I mean, are we sure our evidence is solid on that? It's such an anomaly."

"The Chief was pretty sure he'd caught the guy. Who knew he would have wired his house?" Burke is shaking his head even as I'm speed reading the report.

An ambush at the home of a man named Lou Fitzgerald. It killed Chief Booker and wounded two others. And, Fitzgerald is still at large. A loose description of the man is sketched on the board. Over six feet, bearded, hair clipped short, a tattoo on his upper forearm sketched out and added to the profile.

Four murders since then, and the fifth, the survivor, is in a coma in the hospital.

We need to catch this guy. And apparently, I'm in charge.

I take another sip of coffee. It's bitter but I don't care. "When is the press conference?"

Burke checks his watch. "Three o'clock. So you have some

time."

Time to get up to speed on a case that I've clearly spent thousands of hours and a number of years developing. Fantastic.

"Where is the survivor?"

"She's at the University hospital."

I finish off my coffee. "Okay. I'm on my way."

Burke nods, but a look on his face puts a burr under my skin. "What?"

"Eve will be at the press conference, also, in case there are any questions she needs to answer."

I turn my expression to stone because frankly, that's how my chest feels. "That's not a problem, Burke."

He nods again. "Maybe tonight, we go a round down at Quincy's?"

Quincy's, the boxing gym in north Minneapolis where Burke and I sort out our cases, problems and, once upon a time, my breakups with Eve. I have to wonder how much time I've spent there lately. And if any of the bags have Silas O'Roarke's smug face on them.

Last I remember, he was married, had a daughter named Cyra. So what was he doing here this morning with my wife? His arm clenched around her shoulders looked like more than moral support, but then again, I believe that Silas has always been waiting in the shadows, ready to swoop in.

Apparently, I've cobbled together a make-shift desk in the corner on a long folding table littered with empty coffee cups, file folders and a laptop. I collect the cups, dump them, sit on the office chair, and dig through the files. Names and faces, with detailed officer and forensic reports. No one looks familiar, except one, a female.

Gretta Holmes. The teenager from my box of cold case files in my office at home. Only this one contains a post-it note in Booker's hand. Victim number one?

Maybe he's figured out something I haven't, and added her to our pile of victims.

The one file that's missing, however, is the only one I currently care about. I get up and go to Burke's office, trying to figure out words that don't sound desperate.

Yeah. Right. Who am I kidding?

Burke is sitting in Booker's old office, the one he had when he was Deputy Chief of Investigations. I take a breath, keep it casual. "Hey, Burke, where's Ashley's file? I think I misplaced it." I stick my hands in my pockets, give him a smile.

He knows me better than this. "Nope. I took it."

I take a breath because he's staring me down and I don't want to throw down right here in his office, but—

His hand goes up to stop me. "You've looked at it enough."

Huh?

Burke gets up, comes around, and sits on the edge of his desk. "Rem. Why do I feel I have to remind you we've already had this conversation? It's not your case, and yes, I know Booker thought it was related to the Jackson murders, but that was just a hunch, one that was...it wasn't good for you—"

"What's good for me is trying to figure out what happened to my daughter!" So much for playing it cool. I sense pieces of myself fracturing and I school my voice.

And, I close Burke's door.

He raises an eyebrow.

"Listen. I just need..." I blow out a breath. "I can't remember everything and...C'mon man. Let me see her file."

Burke shakes his head, and a darkness pools in my gut, something that I thought I'd outrun long ago.

The kind of darkness that seeded rumors that may or may not be true about my early days. Only Eve knows what really happened, because she's the one who helped me corral the darkness, dam it up inside, hoping the pond might drain.

Clearly not.

"Burke."

He stands up.

Burke is taller than me, and before he joined the force, he was in the army, so he doesn't flinch easily. He stares at me, his jaw hard. "I know how hard this has been for you. You had everything—your wife, your child, your job—and then it imploded. And yes, you could have handled it differently, but I could have also. I should have pulled you from the case long ago—"

"Give me my daughter's file. Now." My voice is almost a growl.

"No. I can't—"

"She wasn't your kid!"

His jaw flickers. Then his voice softens. "Okay. But not here. Not now. I need your focus on today's press conference. Besides, yesterday was hard enough, don't you think?"

Yesterday. I'm frowning. But we had a birthday party two days ago, so, "You mean her birthday?"

"No," he says quietly, and my gut twists with his tone. "What's going on with you, man?"

And then I remember his words, and speak them even as I remember them. "Yesterday was the anniversary of her death."

He nods as the words hit me, and now my gut is a stone.

Burke gives me a face that tells me that even he is broken by this date. "I told Eve the timing wasn't good, but she was struggling too. I think she just needs this to be over."

This. Her family. Her memories. Us.

"Me too," I say, meaning something completely different.

I turn toward the door. "I hate John Booker for what he did." I'm not sure where that comes from, because frankly, I'm usually not that raw with my feelings, but it's better than putting my fist through the glass of the door.

Burke leans his bulk toward me. "What did you say?"

I round on him. "This is all Booker's fault. If he hadn't given me that box of cold cases—" And I can't continue if I hope to keep Burke from walking me out the front door. Or calling 9-1-1.

I need that file. I need this job.

I need something to hold onto.

"What are you sayin' man? John and you were best friends, all the way to his death. You spoke at his funeral. Not two days ago you told me that you wished you had half his investigative instincts."

His words stymie me, and strangely, elicit a bloom of warmth inside that I can't quite place.

Oh, God, it might be hope.

Because my greatest regret—up until this morning at least—was that John Booker, my mentor and I, parted with wrath between us.

"Oh," I say.

"What cold cases?" Burke asks now.

I shrug, keep my voice easy. "I'm just frustrated that the Jackson killer is still on the loose." I can still lie fast and hard when I need to. Spent about a decade undercover proving that, but it's something Eve doesn't like me to talk about.

Burke is nodding, so I clearly still got it. "Yes. And, didn't you say that you might have found his first victim, according to Booker's last notes?"

I nod too. If you say so.

Burke's phone rings and he pulls out his cell. I make to leave but he holds up his hand. "It's Sams."

Kid brother Mulligan. I make a face because it hits me. "Danny's birthday party. It's tonight."

Danny Mulligan held a birthday party every year and invited his entire precinct. After his death, Bets still held the bash in his honor. I've never missed it, to my knowledge. How could I? Danny was Eve's father, and an icon in the force.

Burke is nodding. "I can tell him you're not going."

"She probably wouldn't want me there," I say to him, to his conversation with Sams.

Burke makes a face, but I pull the door closed behind me and stand in the hallway, the sense of loss bitter in my mouth.

Around me, in the bullpen, a few of my colleagues—some familiar, some not—are eying me like I might be made of diesel and ammonium nitrate.

C'mon, give me a break. I think I'm holding it together rather well.

But if I don't get some answers…

And then it hits me.

I know exactly who can sort this out.

CHAPTER 3

The 1930 Tudor home of watchmaker Arthur Fox is still standing, a couple blocks west of Water street in Stillwater, and I pause at the corner, just taking in the changes.

The first time I saw it, it had a vintage Japanese Maple, in bloom, in the front yard and Hosta that lined the walk. Aged but still stately, a little like its owner, Art, who refused to let me in and told me only that my broken watch was clearly working.

Clearly. Because I saw him again twenty years earlier, and the next day, when said watch began to tick. Art still wasn't the warmest coat in the closet, but I met his wife, Sheila, who turned out to be a real peach and offered me lemonade without enough sweetener in it.

That time, Art left me with the same cryptic words from the back of the watch, Be Stalwart.

I remember the lemonade as I stare at the house and the addition of a wheelchair ramp at the front steps.

The fist is back in my stomach as I approach.

The air is still, cicadas buzzing as if in warning. A shift of the wind reaps the fragrance of hydrangeas nearby.

I ring the bell.

It bellows deep in the house, something mournful and appropriate. The inner door opens and the bars on the outer door dissect a woman's body. "Can I help you?"

She's in her mid-twenties, maybe, with blonde hair, cut short, and kind eyes. She's wearing a pair of yoga pants and a t-shirt, her feet bare.

I'm jarred, and for a second, I lose my words. Maybe Art doesn't live here—

"Meggie, who is it?"

The voice is gnarled, crabby and I'm so relieved I even smile. "I'm looking for Arthur Fox."

She considers me. "Why?"

"I need to talk to him about my broken watch."

"Dad doesn't fix watches anymore." She cocks her head, folding her arms over her chest.

"He'll fix mine." I don't mean to be rude, but really, this is between Art and me. And Father Time, apparently.

"I highly doubt that," Meggie says.

"Meggie, who is it?"

"Some guy who wants you to fix his watch—"

"Be Stalwart. Tell him that."

She rolls her eyes and leaves, shutting the door.

Huh. Like father like daughter, because I'm standing on the stoop without a clue what to do.

I'm about to knock again when the door reopens. "He remembers you. You can talk to him, but not for long. He's tired."

He didn't sound tired when he was shouting at her from across the house, but I bite my tongue and head inside.

Twenty years and a couple days ago, the house was beautiful. Dark crown moldings and arched doorways, gleaming narrow planked pine wood flooring that hosted leather overstuffed chairs and a piano in the corner.

Not anymore.

The piano is still there, but the furniture is mostly gone, and sitting in the middle of the room, staring at a box television, is a man I barely recognize.

He's in a wheelchair and the ramp suddenly makes sense.

Art is just as frail as before, but his back is bowed and his hands sit on the arms of the chair like an afterthought. A belt circles his chest, holding him in place. He's wearing a pair of sweatpants and a shirt that sags over his bony frame.

The redolence of pipe smoke is gone, but I do pick up the faint odor of ammonia and antiseptic. A bag hangs beside his chair.

What happened?

He looks at me, and something sparks in those eyes. They widen and his mouth opens. "Stalwart?"

"Yeah." I walk over beside his chair. "It's me. How are you?" Except, what a terrible thing to ask. I offer a thin smile.

"Did you change anything?"

So he does remember. Our last conversation, the one in the past included me blurting out a diatribe of confusion about my time travel, the fear I might be stuck in the past forever, and too many unanswered questions about how the watch works.

He had no answers. Just the cryptic, The watch is working.

Which is why I nod. "Yes." I have to tighten my jaw against a rush of emotions. I stare at him, and he meets my eyes, and nods slowly.

I can't think, don't have words. I just go to one knee and lower my head.

Deep inside, I fear that somehow, I've done this terrible thing to him. Somehow my choices have created a dissection of time, splintering off to this hell we both find ourselves trapped inside.

I finally take a shuddered breath and lift my head.

Only then do I notice his daughter, seated on the remaining leather chair across the room. A tear falls off her chin. She wipes it fast and gets up, heads into the kitchen.

I turn to Art. "I don't know what to do."

He's listening, and apparently doesn't think I'm certifiable, so, "I used the watch, and it...it sent me back to 1997."

He doesn't blink, unfazed.

"I thought it was a dream at first—it felt like a dream. But I could smell and taste things, so it couldn't be a dream, right? But still, I thought it might be—even until the end. I came back and I was in exactly the same place I was when I left—like I'd never been gone at all. And I still would have thought it was a dream if..." And my throat starts to clog, but I press through, "If my entire world hadn't changed."

I take a breath because his gaze is on me. My voice collapses. "I came home and terrible things have happened to my family. My daughter was murdered. And my wife..." I clench my jaw and force the words. "She's divorcing me."

"Oh, Rembrandt," he says, and gives me a look I want to interpret as sympathy.

But I'm not done, so I clear my throat and keep dishing out the horror. "There's a serial killer on the loose, which is new. I mean, there were kids disappearing before I left—" And even as I say that, I realize that yes, the day I went back to 1997, my wife returned from work with the horrific news of a young man who'd gone missing. Which doesn't match the M.O. on the board, but maybe in this timeline, Booker—and I?—have discovered a connection to the killings.

The Jackson killer.

Or, did I do something in the past to unleash these murders? The idea turns me cold.

I look back at Art. "I don't understand. I mean, how can I do something that causes so many deaths. All I did was solve a cold case."

Art nods.

"You could have rewritten your timeline," says a voice from the door and I realize Meggie has been listening. She's holding a lemonade and now brings it into the room and hands it to me. "Right, Dad?"

"Maybe," Art says.

"What are you talking about?" I say as Meggie comes in and sits down.

"Have you ever heard of Chronothesia?"

"No."

Art pipes up. "It's the idea that we can 'travel' in our minds to a previous time, and in that moment, re-evaluate our actions. It's a way for psychologists to help trauma sufferers re-enact their trauma for a better outcome."

And now he's lost me. "I thought you were a watch repair man."

"I am." But for the first time, ever, I get the tiniest smile from Art.

"Mom and Dad were time travel theorists," Meggie says, warmth in her voice.

"I still am ... maybe," Art mutters.

Meggie glances at my lemonade. I wonder if she's laced it with something stronger. I take a drink and it's tart and bracing and exactly what I need when she adds, "Think mental time travel."

I raise an eyebrow. Because, well, that makes a little sense. "Like... Quantum Leap?"

31

Art chuckles. "No. That was fiction."

Right. "You're saying when I was back in time, I was in my younger body, but my, um, self, stayed here."

Meggie looks at me with something of a bingo in her eyes. "It's the theory that a person could connect with himself, in the past, through chronothesia and create different choices, which would, then affect his current situation."

"Like that movie, Back to the Future."

"Again, that's fiction, but yes you're getting closer."

"You're saying that if I travel back in time in my mind, and relive my life, only with a different outcome, I'm really rewriting my life?"

I look at Art, who is nodding.

"But then I've overwritten all the events of everyone's lives," I say to Meggie.

Now it's her turn to nod.

I steal a furtive glance at Art. How can I reveal what I did to him?

His mouth tightens, however, because he knows that I know something.

"So, what happens to my memories when I come back? If I've changed things, then why don't I remember them?"

"Because your consciousness travels outside of time. Think of it like flying. Then, when you return to your time, the place you started, you 'come back to earth'." Art finger quotes the words. "And once you land, your memories will start catching up. The longer you're in the current time, the more your beginning memories will sync with your new memories."

Which means the longer I stay here, the more my Ashley, my seven-year-old cherub, vanishes. I breathe out low and long. "So how did this happen?"

"Were you thinking about anything specific when you, um, went back?" Art asks.

The cold case. "I was holding a file on the coffee shop bombings. And I went back to the moment of the first bombing."

"So, the connection is your cold cases," Meggie says.

"Those contain some pretty powerful regrets, I'm guessing." Art is looking at me, something of compassion in his eyes.

I nod.

"So powerful, that you might wish yourself back there, to do something different."

I see where he's going. "And that desire could be powerful enough to cause chronothesia?"

"Maybe," Art says.

"And the watch?"

"My theory is that it acts like the GPS system, taking you to the right place and time," Art says.

"But it doesn't even work." I pull back my shirt sleeve to reveal the watch, the hands still frozen.

"Doesn't it?" Art says.

Oh, right...

I have to ask the question but am terrified of the answer. "Can I reset it? Fix it?"

I need my world back.

"Where did you get the watch?" Meggie asks, leaning forward.

"His boss." I can't believe Art remembers that. "The police chief."

Silence.

"Please tell me I can fix what I've done." I sound desperate, because, well, I am.

More silence.

"Art?"

"I don't know. Maybe. But remember, if you try to rewrite time, you risk changing a trillion other tiny elements that can have dire consequences."

Hello. This isn't news to me.

"You could go back and put right what went wrong." Meggie says, her gaze on her father.

"I saved lives," I say. "I can't go back and…blow up the coffee shop."

Although if I could, would I? Right now, maybe I would, although I'm ashamed to admit it.

"I think it's not a matter of fixing, but of creating a rewrite you can live with…" Meggie says. "Or," and she lifts a shoulder, "Maybe you just stay here, and try and live with your new reality."

No. Way.

"How would I even…" And then it comes to me… I'll return to the day Ashley was killed and stop it. I don't care about the cold cases—I mean, yes, I do, but really, what would you do? I'll just change this one thing.

And then, everyone will live happily ever after.

I'm getting my daughter and my wife back. I get up, run my hand over my head and look down at Art. I have to know. "What happened?"

He makes a face. "We were coming back from a wedding on a Saturday afternoon and a car just came out of nowhere and t-boned us."

He glances at Meggie.

"Mom was killed instantly." She puts a hand on his shoulder. "Dad suffered a fracture of his C-4 vertebrae."

I know enough to recognize the injury of a quadriplegic.

"I'm so sorry."

"It was a freak accident. I don't think it's anything you did, son."

Art's words are so kind, I am undone. Especially since this is not the Arthur Fox I remember. Suffering has softened his rough edges.

"Would you like to stay for lunch?" Meggie asks after a pregnant moment.

"I can't. I have to interview a witness and do a press conference."

Meggie glances at the television and back to me. "I thought I recognized you. You're the one who's heading up the investigation on the serial killer."

I freeze, deer in the headlights.

Art is looking at me. "You don't remember that, do you?"

I shake of my head.

"Oh boy," Meggie is shaking her head, too.

Exactly.

"Be stalwart," Art says and I suddenly understand the inscription. Indeed. I head toward the door.

Meggie grabs it behind me as I step out.

I realize I'm still holding the lemonade and finish it before I hand her the glass. "Tastes just like your mother's."

Her mouth opens.

I wink and go to my car.

I think I can fix this.

But first, I have to lie to the world.

CHAPTER 4

I don't know why I find myself parked outside the Mulligans' house, the sun flaming out against the deep blue of Lake Minnetonka. A slight wind bullies the poplar and oak and hovers over the neighborhood, as if in foreboding, and I'm not a detective for nothing. I have instincts and they tell me this is a bad idea.

I'm listening to the radio, the classic rock station, because even in this altered reality I know good music. The kind of music that fueled all my bravest decisions. My Porsche is purring, ready for a getaway.

Queen is singing Crazy Little Thing Called Love. Thank you, Freddie. Because I saw Eve go in earlier and I'm stuck in the what-ifs.

What if Burke is right?

I know you're thinking, about what? Wait for it, I'll explain.

After leaving the Foxes', I headed back to Minneapolis and stopped off at the University of Minnesota to check on Hollie Larue, the latest victim. Some passers-by found her half-drowned in the river near the 35W bridge. A waitress from Mahones, she's blonde, pretty, in her early twenties, and fits the profile of the

Jackson victims exactly. Beaten, sexually assaulted and strangled, with a twenty dollar bill tucked in her fist, the words, "Thank you for your service," written in black sharpie across Jackson's face.

Disgusting, if you ask me. Worse, I can't eject from my brain (although I'm trying) the idea that something this horrific happened to Ashley.

Maybe Burke is right to keep the file away from me.

No. Not for a second. I will wrench that file from him tomorrow, even if it takes a brawl.

I talked with Hollie's parents, a nice suburban couple who deserved better for their youngest daughter. I left my card and asked them to call me if she woke up, then landed back at the precinct and spent the rest of the day cramming for my big show.

Burke loaned me his jacket and I realized I needed to hit the weights a little more. But I put on my game face — the one that has walked into hundreds of gruesome murder scenes, the one that has delivered brutal news to parents — and held a short but succinct briefing in the press room at the precinct, the sun hot on the windows. No details, just the update from the doctors on Hollie and our investigation. Which sadly is nothing, and I again asked people to be careful.

I haven't mentioned the profiles—young, blonde teens and twenty-somethings, most of them waitresses, bartenders, and working girls. And never would I leak the tidbit about the twenty dollar tips. But I advise all young women to stay in the daylight, walk with friends and make wise choices.

It sounds like something I'd say to Ashley when she became a teenager. Becomes. Becomes a teenager.

Apparently, I wasn't a complete train wreck because Burke gave me a nod. I didn't take any questions, but Eve fielded a few about the facts we could release about Hollie. Where she was found, and when. Her condition.

When I stepped back and let Eve take the podium, my heart nearly imploded in my chest.

Her fragrance hit me, and I realized that in my universe, the one I'm desperately missing, tonight we'd be barbecuing burgers and sharing a cold beer under the stars, waiting for Ashley to go to sleep.

And then...

I focused on a spot on the back of her head and tried not to think anymore.

But she looked good. Wore the same outfit as when she met me at the door this morning—dress pants, a crisp white shirt. Her curly auburn hair is tied back, and she has donned a suit jacket, every inch the award-winning forensic scientist.

I also know the other Eve. The one who kicks off her heels when she gets into my car, pulls the band from her hair and un-buttons that shirt low enough for me to remind myself to keep my eyes on the road. I could nearly hear her laughter, soft, light and uncoiling the stress of my day—which, until recently consisted of staring at a blank page in my office, searching for words.

My nose-diving writing career is the very last thing I care about right now.

So, no, not much success in turning my thoughts blank.

When she finished, Eve met my eyes with a tight-lipped half-smile of approval.

I'm like a puppy to her smile, and it took everything inside me not to rush up to her. I feel noosed by the accusations she—and Burke—have thrown at me. I don't know what I did, but I am sure it merits her anger. After all, I know myself. Had a front row seat of the man I was before she married me.

Like I said, I'm surprised she stayed with me this long.

It doesn't make my sucking chest wound bleed less.

She left without a word to me, despite the smile, and frankly it didn't bode well for tonight's party.

"I told you she doesn't want me there," I said this to Burke two hours later as we sparred in one of the two rings at Quincy's.

The old warehouse-turned-gym is located in the heart of Minneapolis and made for guys like me who need loud music and sweat at the end of a day.

Def Leopard had my number as Foolin' blared from the overhead speakers, bouncing against the metal beams and exposed piping as we circled each other.

Burke's mitt grazed my chin, but I jerked back before it could connect, then closed in for a jab to his mid-section. Connected.

I didn't know why his grunt felt so good, but I followed with another and he caught me and shoved me away. He was breathing hard, a sweat turning his bowling ball head shiny. "What did you want her to do? She just delivered you divorce papers." He bounced away from me.

I hit the ropes and came back at him. "I dunno. It's just that Danny and Asher's deaths were at the center of why we came together. She was obsessed with the investigation."

"And you helped her."

"Of course I did. And not just because she was hot."

Burke shook his head as I charged him. But he stopped me with a gloved fist to my jaw. The world blinked and I dropped like a stone.

Shoot.

He laughed as he grabbed me around the arm and pulled me to my feet. "But, she does need you today, even if she says she doesn't."

I don't know what he knows, but those words rang inside me

and I debated, but finally took a shower, headed home, changed clothes, and turned up here.

The night is cool, the sky bruised and hurting and it conjures up the time we—well, she—sneaked into her house to talk her brother, Asher, into helping us crack the coffee shop bombing case. Asher was young and smart and would have made a dent on this world had he and his father not been gunned down at a local convenience store a few weeks later in a drive-by shooting.

It was a retaliation by a gang-boss for Danny's on-the-job killing of his kid brother. At least, those were the whispers on the street. The shooters were never apprehended.

It occurs to me that it's another cold case, one that is providentially sitting in my box of cold files back home.

The deaths of her father and brother unraveled Eve. It skimmed too close to the loss of her best friend, Julia, and for years she obsessed over their killers. She never handled the grief well and stumbled into her own method of mourning. Booker's name was scrawled on the paperwork, but I ran the case and made the decision to file it away in the cold case basement, just trying to keep Eve sane. In a way, Ashley saved her—us, really. Eve finally loosed her grip on justice—or maybe vengeance, we never really got to the bottom of that—and started to embrace peace.

I have to wonder if Ashley's death has loosed the darkness.

It's the memory of her late nights that propels me out of the Porsche and into her driveway. The way she used to twist her hair when she was thinking until it was coarse, fragile, and broken at the ends, the bone-weary fatigue she carried, and the season she spent way too many late nights with Silas.

In those early days, I had to pry her from her lab, but even after that, when the anniversary of their deaths came around, I'd find her holed up, needing rescue.

The twenty-year impulse to save my wife doesn't die with a flimsy stack of divorce papers, now currently dumped in my recycling bin.

Find the beginning. Overwrite.

I want my world back.

My wife back.

The door squeals on its hinges as I reach the front stoop and I stop just inside the pool of light on the bottom step, next to a pot of geraniums.

Samson Mulligan stands in the door frame wearing a pair of jeans and an oxford, the sleeves rolled up like he's ready to rumble.

Perfect. Sams is a real estate investor, but before that, he ran a construction company and has the abs and biceps to prove it. Golden brown hair, blue eyes and a charmer, even now, Sams is single, although I wouldn't be surprised to find a Miss Someone at the gig.

Usually, Sams and I get along. He's Eve's closest brother, so we have some history, back in the day when Eve and I were off and on. Let's remember the idiot part, so I don't blame him. Much. But we threw down once, early in the game, right after Danny's death, which was more about Sams' frustration than anger, but I have an extensive memory. It's an asset in my long game as a detective. Not so much when it comes to family.

Still, I get how the accumulative roil of helplessness might make a person do something crazy.

I take a breath.

So does he. "Eve said you were sitting out there."

She did? I shrug.

"She told me to come out here and...well, if you're drunk, buddy, you're not coming in."

Drunk? "Not even an Irish coffee." I hold up my hands. "Z,

Y, X and W. V, U, T—"

"Get inside." Sams holds the door open, his mouth a tight line, and I can't tell if he's hiding a smile.

"Thanks." I stop at the top steps, however, and lower my voice. "How is she?"

Sams frowns, as if the question throws him. "How are you?"

Me? Confused. Angry. "Sorry," I say.

"Good. No trouble tonight, okay?"

"Scouts honor."

"You were never a scout, Rem." But he lets his smile surface and for a moment I feel normal.

I give a quick glance around. I've always loved the Mulligan house. It faces the lake with a wide bank of windows, through a massive great room added on when Elizabeth Mulligan took a sledge to the wall in her kitchen. A former farmhouse from the early 1900s, it creaks and whines like an old man in winter when the wind off the lake harasses it, but with its vintage oak trees and heirloom Hosta-lined stone walk, the place nets easily in the seven digits. Bets, as Danny called her, is holding onto her family's inheritance with an iron grip, despite Sams' urging to sell and buy a nice condo in Excelsior.

I am not looking forward to the rumble her passing will cause in the family.

She's the iron will, the gale wind, the plumb line, and the voice of truth that holds this family together after the tragedy that landed on them nearly twenty years ago. She's also the one I need to convince that I'm not the guy—not really—who needs a breathalyzer before entering the Mulligan house of refuge.

I can't imagine what would make me turn into the kind of man I have always despised except…again, maybe Burke is wise to keep that file from me.

Maybe.

Chips and dip, fruit plates, vegetable platters, and a tray of Bets' homemade brownies line the giant island that separates the kitchen from the great room. The room is filled with faces I recognize and a few guys raise their hands to me. Among them are the rookies, as if coming is a rite of passage.

They'll hear about Investigator Danny Mulligan who brought down a Brotherhood drug lord, saved a little girl in a fire before the FD arrived, tracked down the toddler son of a state senator in a cornfield, and apprehended a mall shooter before he could finish the havoc he'd come to wreak.

Danny was a hero, and I very much wanted him to like me. But I was a little too brash to realize that before he passed and I'm not sure we got that far.

I regret that.

"You made it." Burke hands me a beer but I shake my head and reach for a Diet Coke. He looks impressed and sets the bottle back into ice. He nods toward the television and I see my mug on the news, Eve standing behind me. She's watching me with an enigmatic look I can't place.

"Think she's serious about those divorce papers?" I don't know why I'm asking Burke, but maybe he's got insider information on this woman I suddenly don't know.

"She's left them three times since…well, since …" Burke swallows. "So yeah, I think she's serious."

"I need to know why."

"My guess is that she's tired of waiting. She needs to start over."

Then tonight's the night, because I've never been more serious about restarting my life.

Although, my plans include a different kind of restart. As soon as I get my hands on Ashley's file tomorrow, I'm chronothizing (my word, but remember, I'm also a novelist and we make up words) my way to a new reality.

Right now, however, I'm going to repair some bridges so that should things go south, I have something to come back to.

I wander over to a side table, heavy with framed pictures of the family. Asher is grinning, wearing a stocking hat over his long reddish brown 90's hair, gesturing a hang ten into the camera. In another, Danny is holding a walleye on a stringer, one arm around an annoyed teenage Samson. In a smaller snap, Lucas and Jake sit on a picnic table eating watermelon.

My gaze, however, fixes on the one of Eve sitting in one of the backyard Adirondack chairs, on her dad's lap. She has her arms looped around his neck, and looks about fourteen, all long auburn hair, gangly legs and buck teeth.

My heart nearly explodes. I'm not sure how I'm going to return home tonight to my barren house, memories lurking in every corner.

The picture is in my hand, my thumb running down Eve's countenance when I feel a grip on my arm.

It's Bets and I'm caught, frozen. "Rem."

I put the picture down. "Bets. I..." And I'm not sure what to say. She's wearing a sleeveless top and a pair of white jeans, her bobbed blonde hair tucked behind her ears and a simple gold chain at her neck. She hasn't taken her wedding ring off since the day Danny died, and I get it.

I stare at her, I can't help it. Eve is my heart and soul. I probably always knew that, despite the denial in my youth and I wish I'd been an honest man from the beginning. But I'm here now and as God is my witness, I'm not going to give her a reason to leave me the second time around.

I put all that in my eyes as I fail to find words.

"I'm glad you're here, Rem. Eve is outside." Bets gestures past me, to where the twilight has draped the night in hues of deep purple. Eve is an outline on the family picnic table. Bets squeezes my arm. "Danny liked you."

I think that's a lie, but I'm not man enough to argue with Bets.

I pick up another soda on the way out.

The air is warm and rich with the ebullience of summer as it lifts off the lake. It stirs memories of skinny dipping, sailing and all the early days with Eve, when fun and games were the only items on the agenda.

I stop at the table.

Eve has changed into a pair of jeans and a white tee shirt, her auburn hair loosened and wild in spirals around her face. I mentally twirl my finger through one of those corkscrews, but hold myself back.

My Eve wouldn't mind, and this one so resembles the woman I know that for a moment I believe in fresh starts and happy endings.

Then she looks over at me. Weariness is etched in the lines around her eyes. She's been crying, and she plays with the tiny heart charm on her gold necklace, the one her father gave her for her sixteenth birthday.

I did this. Art is right—something I did derailed us into this terrible vortex of grief. Right now, I should be tucking my daughter into her bed, singing her a terrible version of You are My Sunshine.

But this is the reality I'm in, and I'm going to leave it better than I found it. So, "Can I join you?" I hold out the soda.

Eve wipes her cheeks and nods, the sadness in her eyes so deep it punches a hole through me.

I slide up beside her. She smells vaguely of the perfume I tried to ignore today. Now, I let it sift into my pores, let it devour me.

"Pretty sunset." I'm referring to the last simmer of magenta along the lip of the lake.

"Mmmhmm." She opens the can.

"Good turnout." I inwardly groan. I'm a writer. I can do better than this. We've been married for nearly ten years. I know Eve. I know how she thinks, and how to make this better, so, "The point of reopening cold cases is to use new technology to solve old crimes. The only reason we couldn't nail Danny and Asher's killers is that we never got a good look at them. They drove by too fast to see the footage in the convenience store camera. But maybe we pull the tapes, digitize them, slow them down, let the computer fill in the variables...?"

She doesn't respond for a full ten seconds. Finally she takes a sip of the Diet Coke then says, "The only reason we didn't get them is because they weren't the ones who pulled the trigger." She gives me a quick glance. "The real murderer is Hassan Abdilhali, head of the Brotherhood, but no one will give him up."

Hassan now runs one of the biggest Somali gangs in the city while under the disguise as a legitimate businessman who owns a string of laundromats. He sits on the council board of an outlying northern suburb.

"There are men serving nickels and dimes right now, that were members of the Brotherhood in '97. How many wood panel station wagons could there be in 1997? I could take another crack at them—"

Her hand slips onto my wrist. It's warm and firm and she squeezes. "There's nothing we can do about it, Rem. Some things we just need to learn to accept."

I don't want to ask, but does that include the destruction of our marriage?

Staring out at the lake, I fall to quiet. The dark waves ripple against the sandy beach, make a thumping noise against an over-turned canoe.

"Ash loved the lake," I say, not sure why, but I'm caught in a memory. "Remember that time she raced down the dock without stopping and flew right into the water? She dropped like a rock—"

"She was two. If you hadn't been there to grab her..." Eve looks over at me and she's wearing a ghost of a smile. I want to reach up and wipe away the glistening on her cheek.

"She wasn't the least scared of water, not even after that. Last summer, she swam all the way out to the floating dock—"

I feel her body go stiff. "What?" Her breathing catches.

I pull in my own quick breath. "I mean, the last summer, she was...um..." And there's no getting out of this because I don't remember Ashley's last summer.

She's still alive, to me.

"Are you okay?" Eve frowns and I draw in another breath.

Maybe there's room for a sliver of truth. "No. I'm not okay. I keep having these..." and I don't want to freak her out, so, "visions that Ash is still alive. She's happy and seven years old and just had a birthday party in our back yard." And I want her to believe me, to just somehow reach into my brain and see the reality that we just had—maybe can have again if I do this right. "She got ponies and a castle, and more of those stupid stuffed animals, and I spent the entire weekend building her a swing set..."

Her eyes are filling again.

"And I finally found Gomer..."

She wears a sad look. "Rem. You know...you know visions are just visions, right?" It's like she's talking to a child. To Ashley, telling her that there are no monsters under her bed.

But there are monsters, the kind that will slink out after I go home and find me, remind me that if I can't figure this out, then this is the world I'll have to live in. "I know. It's just…it feels like it could be real."

She presses her hand to my cheek. "No amount of drinking is going to make that happen."

Wow. I must have really taken a dive. "The drinking is over."

She draws in a breath. Drops her hand.

Good bet is I've said that before. "I promise, Eve. I'm not the man who finished off that bottle of Macallans in the recent past. I'm different. Really. I'm…I'm me."

She closes her eyes, as if my words pain her. "You have no idea how much I want to believe that, Rem."

"Then—"

"It's too late." She opens her eyes. "I didn't just lose Ashley when she died you know. I lost you too. Your obsession with finding the guy … then your drinking …"

She trails off, the pain in her eyes searing into my heart.

I stare at her, seeing, for the first time, how we got here. I've never been good at letting go, at living with questions and helplessness. The search for questions about my missing brother is why I became a detective.

Another tear escapes and she catches it with her hand. "I have no hope left, Rem. I have to move on."

Move…on? "With Silas?"

At my statement, a horror enters her eyes, and I'm so relieved, I barely hear her when she says, "With my life. The one without Ashley."

Ah, that kind of moving on.

"The one without you." It comes out in a whisper.

Anyone else feel the sucking chest wound? I even make a sound, deep inside. My voice betrays it. "You don't have to move on from me," I say. "Please, Eve."

Her countenance falls and for a second, I think she'll change her mind. There's something desperate in the gaze that roams my face. I know this look.

"Eve." I lean toward her reaching up to touch her cheek. "I love you. We have been through so much together. We can get through this."

She closes her eyes again, and for a moment leans into my hand. Sighs. Then, "Rem, it hurts too much to love you."

I stiffen even as she pulls away.

"And I think that's the point, isn't it? I can't keep living in grief. My father. Asher. Our daughter. And now you. I can't watch you spiral out and destroy yourself. I can't come home again to find you in the bathroom, overdosed. It nearly killed me the first time. I can't...I just... Let's not hurt each other anymore, okay?"

I did what?

She gets off the table. "I should probably give this back to you." Reaching into the darkness, she grabs a file off the table. It's brown and worn, a rubber band around the contents to keep them from spilling out. It was sitting behind her, on the other side of the table. I look at it and make out Booker's handwriting.

Right. The Mulligan file. When she picked it up, I haven't a clue, but I nod slowly. Tuck it under my arm.

She sighs. "Sign the papers, Rem. Let's get this done, for all our sakes."

She walks away, back to the house, into the darkness.

And I let her go.

Because tomorrow, I get my family back.

CHAPTER 5

It's not the scream that wakes me. Because, in my dream, I'm expecting it.

In fact, it's not a dream, it's a memory. I can smell fresh cut lawn, hear the sprinkler from Russell's house next door. Inside, Eve is fixing dinner, and she's turned up my Bon Jovi album, singing along to Runaway...

I'm pushing Ashley on her new swing set. Her legs are out, and her braids are flying and she's laughing, screaming, glancing over her shoulder at me, her daddy.

My chest is full. Especially when Eve walks out onto the deck carrying a plate of meat for the now smoking grill. It's a blue-skied day and the heady redolence of the burgers snapping and browning draws me over. I circle my arms around Eve's waist, lean in and press my lips to her neck, her skin tasting of salt and a hint of today's soap. I'm suddenly ravenous, but she hums, then pushes me away, grinning at me over her shoulder, just like Ash did, only not quite. There's a twinkle in Eve's eyes and she winks because it's Saturday night and my world is perfect.

"Rem!"

I turn, looking for the voice, then round back to Eve who has left me for the kitchen.

I follow her inside, but she's not there. "Eve?"

"Rembrandt!"

My head pounds. "Eve?" I walk through our family room, past the wrapped canvas pictures we took at the beach, the long sectional where Ash and I watch Dora and up the stairs to our bedroom.

But it's empty too.

"Rembrandt, are you here?"

I head back downstairs and to my office. It's exactly how I left it—leather chair, rows and rows of novels on a bookcase behind the desk. My novel, The Last Year, in hardcover, on my desk, as if it might give me inspiration.

Eve says she fell in love with me through that book, written my rookie year as an investigator. It hit the NYT Bestseller list, and bought me my Porsche, and a few other toys. I thought I was going to be the next Mickey Spillane. I had no idea what a fluke it was until I attempted novel number two.

I might be a one-hit wonder. But Eve doesn't care, and that's why I'm searching the house for her. Why I'm ignoring the voice... the voice...

The pounding.

I open my eyes, and stare at the ceiling. I'm fully clothed, having dropped onto my sectional last night, one of my mother's knitted afghans over me. I couldn't bear to sleep in the bed Eve and I shared—and will again, I'm determined.

Wow, I miss them.

The voice comes again ... from outside the front door. "Rem, I'm going to call 9-1-1!"

I untangle myself and roll to my feet, still clearing my head, gulping past the thrum of my heart.

I see a figure through the glass and open the door to find my neighbor, Gia. She's wearing a tank top, short shorts and holds her baby on her hip. She's curvy and young and there are sirens sounding in my head, although I'm not sure why.

"Finally," she says. "I was getting worried."

"Sorry. I was sleeping." Dreaming, actually, and I'm not a little irked that she woke me up. I glance past her. Must be around six a.m.—the sun is barely up. Which now has me awake. "What's going on?"

"It's…" And now I realize she's been crying, her eyes reddened. Her baby—I think it's a boy, dark curly hair, big brown eyes—stares at me, his thumb jammed full hilt into his mouth. "Alex. Again."

Alex. The last thing I remember about her husband Alex is the fight he and Gia got into a few weeks ago. Eve and I watched, and I debated crossing the street to intervene. But domestic squabbles are exactly how many cops get shot, so I stayed put and made sure nobody threw anything like chairs or fists.

Alex finally left in his Beemer.

I'm thinking, in this reality, maybe he's not much different.

"Come inside." I hold open the door.

She enters and sets her son down on the floor. He hangs onto her leg, eying me.

"It was so terrible. He came home last night, late, and he'd been drinking and he accused me…" She lifts her gaze to me. "He thinks I'm having an affair."

And, bad me, but all I can think about is Russell, my other neighbor, and how the kid at her feet looks an awful lot like…

I've been a cop too long.

Then Gia takes a step toward me, and suddenly I'm thinking

her husband has grounds because she puts her head on my chest, curls her arms around me, and starts to weep.

Oh. Boy. Uh…

"It's okay, Gia." I pat her back as benignly as I can because right about now is when Eve would arrive and I'd have some 'splainin' to do. I dearly hope I didn't lose my mind and do something colossally stupid over the past three years with the neighbor across the street.

She pushes away from me. "I'm sorry. I just…you and Eve have been so supportive." She wipes her eyes. "I miss her. I hope you two work it out."

Phew. I nod. "Me too."

"I was wondering, maybe, if I could stay here today? Just until Alex leaves? He's sleeping it off on my sofa, but…" She makes a face. "He parked in front of my car, too, and has the keys on him."

Here? In my house?

It won't matter, though, because by the time I'm back, my world will have reverted and Gia will be back to flirting with Russell, single and without junior, so, "Sure. I'm going to take a run, though, and clean up. Why don't you and junior—"

"His name's Mikey."

And that jerks me, just for a second because that was my brother's name.

The one who went missing when I was twelve.

"Oh." I swallow. "So yeah, when I get back from the run—"

"I can make you breakfast." She pushes past me to the kitchen.

Hmmm …

I hear cupboard doors opening. But it's not like I'm doing anything wrong—she's a neighbor in trouble. And clearly, she knows I'm married, so I take the stairs, change into my workout gear and head out the front door, my ear buds in.

My route is always the same. Cut down Drew Avenue, over to Cedar Lake Parkway, then halfway around the lake to the beach, where I do a set of pull ups on the monkey bars of the playground. Sometimes, if no one is looking, I'll drop for some push-ups, too, then run home as fast as I can.

It's a decent, forty-minute workout that keeps my blood pressure down and the tacos from piling up on my waistline. But having recently inhabited my former, rather buff, body, I'm tasting my youth and eager to find it again as I start my route. It's early, the lake is a deep amber thanks to the rising sun, the horizon dark, magenta skies over an explosion of gold, red and orange.

Regardless of the time, the sky is predictable. Sunrise. Sunset. I'm listening to The Four Seasons December, 1963 (Oh, What a Night) and it conjures up my dream.

I'm breathing hard by the time I reach the park. As I do my pullups, I think about Hollie Larue and her parents. And how they'd like to rewrite time. The watch is at home—I took it off yesterday and now the idea of losing it, even to Mikey's chubby handed curiosity propels me back home.

The house is filled with the smells of bacon and eggs when I enter. Laughter rolls out of the kitchen. I walk into my office and grab my watch, still breathing hard.

"You okay?" Gia is in the doorway of the kitchen. I turn and nod. The welcome scent of coffee floats down the hallway, giving me a tug, but I ignore it and head upstairs.

Okay, I was over-reacting. If she needs to stay here to be safe… well, I didn't become a cop to turn people out into the cold.

I shower, change into my last pair of clean jeans and another button-down, put on the watch, and emerge, my shaggy hair back behind my ears, clean-shaven and humming.

Gia's fixed a plate of bacon and eggs for me, and as I walk into the kitchen, she pops it into the microwave. She's also poured me coffee.

As I sip the coffee as fast as I can, the microwave dings and she sets the breakfast on the table. I pick up the plate and shovel in the eggs. "I gotta run." I grab the bacon, though. "You going to be okay?"

She nods. "I'll leave as soon as he does."

There's something about her words that sit in my chest as I get in the Porsche. The idea that maybe, somehow in my relationship with Eve, I left first, at least emotionally.

It happens, especially when I'm writing. Wrap myself up in the fiction, absent in mind, if not in body, for hours, days at a time.

I did it at work, too.

I'll fix that when I reset my world.

Honey, I'm coming home.

I turn on the radio, and my gaze falls on the file folder from last night. The Mulligan file. I shove it into my satchel to look at later, and pull out, heading downtown.

My phone buzzes in the cup holder, and I turn on my Bluetooth. My ride might be vintage, but I tricked it out with all the current technology.

Burke's voice booms through the speakers. "Hollie woke up. Meet me at the hospital."

Aw. Not the item at the top of my agenda, but lives are at stake here, too, and the past isn't going anywhere, so I agree and hang up.

The University Hospital is a sprawling set of buildings seven blocks deep but it has a valet parking service and although it grinds me, I pull up, get a ticket and let some kid take my pretty into the high rise lot while I find Hollie's floor.

Burke is outside the room, leaning against the wall, his arms folded. "It's a miracle. They thought she'd never talk again, maybe not even wake up. But she's awake, coherent, and the doc says you can talk to her for five minutes."

Her parents are in the room, next to her bed. Hollie is still under oxygen, the bruises around her neck deep purple. Her face bears the marks of a struggle, her eye blackened, her lip broken. But she's alive and that's all I can think of as I come up to the bed. She's alive, and twenty-three other women aren't, and if I can catch this guy, then I leave this timeline a safer place.

"Hollie," I say. "I'm an Investigator with the Minneapolis Police Department. Rembrandt Stone. I'm so sorry about what happened to you."

Her eyes film, and I get it. When people understand your pain, it's easier to trust them. Not a technique—I mean the words—but it helps the questions go down easier.

Eve taught me that.

"I'd like to ask you a few questions about your attacker. That okay?"

She nods and out of the corner of my eye, I see her father take her hand.

"Do you remember anything about him? Any description?" We already have the time and place, the details of the attack from Eve's crime scene report. What I need are specifics to help me find, and nail, Leo Fitzpatrick for these murders.

Her breath hiccups and her voice comes out soft and a little hoarse. "It happened so fast. I was coming out of work at Mahones and I heard someone behind me. I started running, and he tackled me. He put his foot in my back and held me down and..." Her eyes are filling. "He told me not to scream, but I did anyway, so he hit me. And then he..." She looks away. "I couldn't breathe." She closes her eyes and I hate that I have to ask her to relive this.

"Do you remember anything, his voice, his smell—"

"Yes." She looks back into my eyes, her gaze searching. "He smelled…like a locker room. Sweaty and foul and…" Her expression matches her words. "He kept talking so quietly the entire time, saying I'm sorry, and Don't scream. He sounded…wounded. Like he was angry that he was hurting me." She shook her head. "I don't remember anything else."

A gym. That's at least, something. "Thank you, Hollie." I meet her father's eyes and I thank him too. "If she remembers anything else…"

He nods, his eyes dark with fury and I feel it in my bones. I get it.

Leo Fitzpatrick killed my daughter, too.

I need to see that file, and I say as much to Burke when I walk out of the room.

He's clearly still on the precipice and I give him a look. "I need to check something," I say, as if the interview has dislodged a clue. "I have a hunch."

His face betrays the fight I might have to have with him.

"Okay. Against my better judgment. I'll get it for you as soon as I get back to the office. I have a meeting, then I need to pick up my car from the shop." He checks his watch. "Could be a while."

I hide a grin. "The Acura finally give up the ghost?"

He's frowning. "Really?"

Whoops. Apparently, we're not driving the boring sedan anymore. "Sorry. Listen. How about I let you use the Porsche. I can take an Uber back to the precinct."

He considers me, but he's always liked my wheels, so I see the yes forming. "Fine. I'll drop you off, then swing by to get you when my car is done."

I won't be there, maybe, but maybe neither of us will, (I'm not sure how this works, exactly), so I nod.

He considers me. "Okay. The file is in my desk. Side drawer. You know the combination."

Huh. So he's still using his military ID number.

"In the meantime, you start shaking down the local gyms."

"Sure thing." Then, I stick out my hand. I'm not sure why, but this Burke has been a good friend to me, and I'll miss him. He stares at me, but shakes it, wearing a frown and a half-grin.

"What?"

"It's just…aw, nothing. Hey." He's still holding my grip. "Is that Booker's watch?" He turns my wrist over.

"Yeah. He gave it to me. Doesn't work though. It's just a momento."

"Did you try winding it? John was always fiddling with it."

I stare at him, a coldness flushing through me. You don't think…did Booker know how to—

"See you back at the precinct," Burke says, breaking through my realization.

I toss Burke the keys, and give him my valet stub, then pull up my app for Uber. My ride is waiting for me when I reach the lobby.

The office is just starting to hum with the day when I arrive, the coffee makers gurgling and cell phones ringing. The bull pen is busy with junior investigators and officers typing out reports. I see an open box of donuts next to the coffee machine and take one. If everything goes right, this version of reality is about to be overwritten.

I head to Burke's office and work the lock. Inside, along with a thick file is a bottle of Dewars, two glasses and a metal lockbox. Interesting. I retrieve the file and take it down the hall to my office.

The Jackson files are piled on my desk. I drop my satchel on the floor and sit down.

Flip off the rubber binder and open the case.

A picture of my four-year old is stapled to the top, along with her case number and maybe Burke was right—I don't want to see this.

But I can't stop a crime if I don't know about it, so I open the file.

The picture assaults me, and I wince, bile filling my chest at the color photograph of Ashley's body, found in a shallow river in Bass Lake park. She's wearing her Little Mermaid nightgown, her feet dirty, her hair tangled as if she'd been dragged.

I swallow the bile back, turn the picture over and read the report. Taken from our home in the middle of the night—where was I?—and found two days later in the park. Strangled.

Not sexually assaulted, however. I close my eyes against a terrible heat. Thank you, God.

But she must have been so terrified. I can almost hear her calling for me and the sound of it echoes in the chambers of my soul.

Enough. I push back my sleeve. Last time I wound the watch it simply ticked to life, soft, a heartbeat through time. Then the hands spun and settled on the time of the first explosion.

But the hands don't move. There's no thunder, no blackness folding over me.

I close my eyes, and try to project myself to Ashley's bedroom, standing amid the neighborhood of stuffed animals, imagine her sleeping in her bed, her blonde hair splayed over her pillow.

I'm still here, and my chest is tightening.

I put my hand on the file, twist the dial again.

Outside the room, someone is yelling, something about an accident.

I'm trying to focus. I let myself go to the park, where she's found, imagine myself standing on the path…

The sound of pounding feet washes over me. One of the

dispatchers has sprinted down the hallway. She sticks her head into the room. "Rembrandt—it's your car!"

My car? I stand up. "What are you—"

"It exploded. Right on the street!"

I stride to the window.

The 911 is in the parking lot, flames licking out of the broken windows, the hood, spiraling black into the sky. Sirens scream in the distance. Officers are trying to approach the car, their hands over their faces to shield them from the heat.

Oh my—"Burke!"

I turn to sprint out of the room, and slam into my table. My files knock to the floor, and on instinct, I turn to catch them, the files, my satchel—all of it as they tumble to the ground.

Forget it. They scatter about and I ignore them, stepping on them as I run toward the door.

I hear thunder, and maybe it's an explosion outside, but the room suddenly starts to tilt, and glass is shattering, and I am falling.

Burke!

Then the locomotive rolls over me, and I plunge face first into time.

CHAPTER 6

I'm not exactly falling because I can still feel my feet beneath me, but there's wind and shouting and my stomach upends.

Then time blinks and I'm standing in the middle of Quincy's, the rank odor of sweat rising around me. Boston is telling me it's more than a feeling through overhead speakers, and I'm trying to find my footing just as a gloved fist slams through my periphery.

I don't have the clarity to duck and the blow lands square on my jaw, knocking me back.

What the—I round on my assailant and swing hard.

It's an uppercut that snaps his head back and he drops like a stone.

"Seriously, Rem. What was that?"

I clear my head and Burke—the young Burke, with the soul patch and hair, his body lean and defined, gets up. "I thought you wanted to play it easy."

It's then I remember the fire, the explosion.

My Porsche, Burke at the wheel. I desperately hope that I'm going to overwrite his death.

"Easy? Then what was that?" I say, trying to buy myself time.

"You let down your guard."

"I…" And probably he's right, so I grind my jaw.

He lowers his hands. "You're still recovering from that stab wound, dude. Let's call it."

Stab wound.

I crane my neck and sure enough, there's the wound, a bright red pucker, on my hip where Ramses Vega's knife slid in behind my kidneys, just missing major organs.

I haven't a clue when I've returned to, although my healing wound is some indication that at least a few weeks have passed since my last visit—Chronosync?—over Memorial Day weekend.

Which means I haven't returned to the time of Ashley's death.

I'm back in 1997. In my twenty-eight year old body, with the moves and the muscle and the ability to whip Burke's sorry backside if I can I untangle my brain.

He's grinning, and I'd really like to clean his clock, so I straighten.

"Call it?" I want to take the body I've missed out for a spin, so I advance on Burke. "Not yet."

I know his moves now, having sparred with him for two decades. Know his tells, the way he feigns left, hits right, and then again. I block his blows and land one in his gut.

Burke is all about longevity. Me, I like slick footwork, body movement and I'm not above covering up to avoid punishment, at least long enough to look for an opening.

Burke loves his power shots. Which means that I have to be on my game or he'll knock me out with a precision punch. I'm more of a pressure guy—lay out the hammer blows until Burke tires. I'm all uppercuts and hooks.

Burke is playing nice with me, I know, because he's avoiding the body shots.

But I'll also take a shot to land one, and it's not long before we're both breathing hard, sweating and hurting.

I grin at him. "Nice to see you again."

He frowns, then, "Ready to tap out?" Sweat drips off his chin.

Yeah, might be, because it's now I realize I'm really hurting. I bend over and grab my knees.

Look up at him.

Burke comes at me again, but he lacks the finesse of his older version and I duck under his arm and grab him around the waist, tackling him down to the floor.

We both roll away, stare at the piping that laces the ceiling, our chests rising and falling.

"What is this, mutually assured destruction?"

I look over at the voice and my heart nearly leaves my chest.

Eve is standing with a friend, and while it's the friend who's spoken, it's only Eve I see. She's carrying a backpack over her shoulder, her kinky auburn hair long and tied back, wearing a pair of jeans and a tee shirt and she's so pretty, so young, and smiling at me and everything inside me wants to crawl over to her and kiss her.

Instead I nod and push myself up to a sitting position. "Hey."

She smiles back, but there's a hesitation in her eyes. "Hey."

Burke has climbed off the floor. "Hey Shelby."

Right. Shelby Ruthers. He dated her for a long time, but eventually she broke his heart with another guy at the station. She's a blonde, curvy and tall, and works in dispatch. If I remember correctly, she worked patrol for three years before applying to investigations. A few times.

"You boys are here early," Shelby says and I glance at the big clock hanging over the office.

6 am. Is that early? Burke and I had a standing 5 am date for a while, before we got old and moved it to post-work.

I look back at Burke. "What's the date?"

He frowns.

"July 2nd," Eve says.

Gretta Holmes. Waitress found dead in an alley outside a diner, killed early in the morning on July 2nd, 1997. One of my cold cases, although Booker had updated it, put it in the Jackson file.

I'm not sure how it happened, but her case has brought me back in time. I hear Meggie's voice. "I think it's not a matter of fixing, but of creating a rewrite you can live with…"

Maybe I don't have to catch Ashley's killer. I just need to reset, overwrite, get on the right timeline, whatever.

I don't know how it works, just that if I do this right, I get my family back.

Which maybe means solving Gretta's case, if I want to reboot my life.

"We gotta go," I say to Burke. According to my sketchy memory, Gretta died of a head injury. Not the MO of the Jackson killers, but maybe Booker knew something.

"Go where?" Burke climbs out of the ring, and Shelby smiles at him and we so don't have time for this.

But what, exactly, am I going to say? I know there's a murder going down, I feel it in my bones? "I need some coffee."

Burke looks at me. "Really?"

It's now I remember that our last big case was the coffee shop bombings, so maybe he's a little skittish. I circle back around with, "I found this great breakfast place, but we have to get there before the specials sell out."

He's still looking at me like I've lost my mind, so I climb out of the ring and head for the locker room.

But not before I turn to Eve for another look. Wow, I'd forgotten how she could blow me away. Somehow, I manage a cool, "You look great, Eve. It's nice to see you."

She offers a smile, as if surprised, and I wonder what the idiot twenty-eight year old me has been up to in my absence.

'C'mon Burke!" He's still flirting with Shelby. She's not worth your time, I want to say, but maybe in this world she is, so I just grab him by the arm and yank him toward the locker room.

We have lives to save.

I'm yelling at him from the shower to hurry up and Burke's annoyed and not just a little confused when he slides into my Camaro five minutes later.

I'm in a suit again. Clearly, I need to write a note to my younger self to loosen up.

Wow, sweet ride, how I've missed you. Right now, my Porsche is sitting in my father's barn waiting for me to check the timing belt. She's running with a hiccup, so I'm guessing the belt has jumped a tooth.

But the Camaro will do. I punch it as we head down Hennepin Avenue to Lulu's.

1997. Not so long ago, but subtle changes have taken place. In my time, the football stadium is gone, replaced by the shiny metallic US Bank stadium of the Vikings. Now, the puffy white covered dome stands in the middle of the city.

I take highway 55, get off at Lake Street and curse the lights that could be costing Gretta her life.

Although, she might already be dead.

We pull up to Lulu's, a 1950's diner on the corner of 41st and Lake. A tattoo parlor sits dark across the street, and next door, barks from the animal clinic suggest the dogs have heard something.

Lulu's sits alone in a weedy parking lot, a gleaming metallic building that conjures up Richie and the gang hanging out at Arnold's diner. I get an image of the Fonz as I park the Camaro.

She's around here, somewhere, and if my memory is correct...

"Did you hear something?" I say over the top of the car.

Burke has gotten out, running a hand over his suit. He raises an eyebrow. "Like? My ears are still ringing."

Oh. I might have played Seger a little too loud, but frankly, nothing pumps the blood more than tracking down a killer to Old Time Rock and Roll.

Or, the fact that I'm settling into a life—my life—like a pair of Levis.

"I thought I heard..." I walk over toward the dumpsters, set at the edge of the lot in front of a wooded area of trash and debris.

She's here. I remember now, and—

"Burke!" I've spotted her.

She's wearing yellow pants, tennis shoes, and a jean jacket and is sprawled face down, as if she'd been running, tackled and left to die. Her brown hair is in a puddle around her, soaked in blood.

I crouch next to her and turn her over.

A massive red and purple hematoma lifts from the side of her head, and a cut has opened, bleeding into her face. She's not breathing. I wipe her mouth with my sleeve and start CPR.

Burke is beside me, calling for 9-1-1.

I'm still compressing, offer her two breaths, and back to the compressions. CPR has been updated since 1997, but I don't remember the early training.

"How did you see her?" Burke says, but I can't answer.

C'mon, Gretta!

I check her pulse. Nothing.

Sirens bruise the morning air and a few people clutter the parking lot, voyeurs to the tragedy in the weeds.

I focus on Gretta. She's still not breathing and I fear—know—the worst. But the fire department has arrived, and with them the rescue squad and a couple of EMTs take over as I back away.

That's when I see it. A twenty dollar bill in her grip. Victim number one? Well done, Booker.

Gretta is young. Eighteen. The only daughter of a couple from the upscale neighborhood of Edina. I dread having to talk to them again—but this time, at least, when I tell them that we'll solve the case, I'll be able to keep that promise.

I hope.

Burke keeps the crowd away, but a woman pushes past him, her hands over her mouth.

I remember her now. Teresa Birch. She wears a full sleeve of tats down her arms, dresses in fifties attire—this morning a hot pink dress—and wears her cherry red hair in victory rolls. Hard to forget. Especially when, in a time before, she offered to give me free breakfasts for life, wink, wink.

I get up and walk away, watching the EMTs do their work. They can't call it until they get her to the Hennepin County Medical Center, but I'll bring in the CSI team and get them started. I know she hasn't been here long.

Someone saw something. In fact, her killer might be standing in the crowd. Which I face and stare down. A few businessmen, construction workers, a couple women.

It starts here. Now.

A Ford escort pulls up, and my body stills as Eve slides out. Shelby emerges from the other side, holding a radio.

Eve walks over to the edge of the crowd, looks at the EMTs working on Gretta. Eve's face is drawn, a frown tangling her expression. Then she meets my eyes, such a sadness in her expression it nearly steals my breath.

It's the same look she gave me last night.

And with a jolt, I know.

I'm not here for Gretta.

I'm here to save Danny and Asher. Because in less than forty-eight hours, they die.

CHAPTER 7

It wasn't Julia. Of course it wasn't, but every time Eve let her imagination snapshot Julia's's body, it looked like this.

Broken, in the weeds, a glassy look to the heavens as if shocked.

She blew out a breath, trying to shake away the grief. Focus. She was on the job after all, not looking at the fifteen-year-old body of her best friend.

Her job was to see what other people missed. She had to detach. Think outside of her emotions. Eve stepped back and took another shot of the victim's body with her Canon EOS3.

"He's freaking me out," said Silas as he blotted blood from the edge of dumpster and dropped the swab into a vial. "He's just standing there like a buzzard, watching us work."

"Who?"

"Your buddy, Stone."

She glanced over her shoulder.

Inspector Stone was watching them, standing at the edge of the crime scene, outside the yellow taped lines, his arms folded over his chest, dressed in a pair of jeans, a pressed oxford and a suit jacket. He needed a shave. Or not.

She'd wanted to go home and change. Thanks to Shelby, she still wore her track pants and a t-shirt, although she'd pulled her CSI vest from Silas's car. Silas was dressed like she should be—in his uniform, a pair of jeans, white shirt, his CSI vest.

"He was stabbed. That probably makes a guy a little pre-occupied with justice," she said, not sure why she was defending him.

She needed to get this stupid man off her brain.

Not that she was making any marked progress. Even now she felt it, the little stir of attraction that would only lead to her noticing how he walked, breathed and shoot, wishing he'd look her way.

Like he did today at the gym.

Stupid Shelby. Of course they'd gone to the gym where Burke worked out. And at o-dark hundred hours, too. Sheesh, the woman was on the trail hard after Burke.

"I can see the appeal," Shelby had said as Rembrandt walked away, glistening with sweat, his dark hair disheveled, wearing a sleeveless shirt and a pair of boxing shorts, all hard-bodied and male. Eve fled to the locker room.

Rembrandt and Burke had left by the time they emerged, but Shelby had Burke on her radar, and after hearing him call in the attack on her scanner, she practically dragged Eve off the elliptical by her hair.

Okay, admittedly, Eve didn't drop to the ground in protest, but still…

Turning away from him, Eve zoomed in on the edge of the dumpster.

The sky was high over the scene, glinting off the metallic diner and gilding the parking lot. An assembly of onlookers had multiplied as the morning drew out. Burke and Rem had interviewed most of the patrons from the diner, as well as any other onlookers while she waited for Silas to arrive in their CSI truck.

"He's pre-occupied with your backside," Silas muttered, bagging some hairs found wedged into the edge of the dumpster.

Oh, hardly. Because he hadn't exactly gone out of his way to find her after he was released from the hospital a month ago.

She felt like a fool, running to the hospital and sitting in his room like a groupie, or worse, a girlfriend, after he'd been stabbed. Sure, he'd been pale and broken, hooked up to oxygen, but when he'd opened his eyes and looked at her, he acted like he barely knew her.

Or didn't want to?

So what—they'd shared a kiss.

Okay, not just a kiss. Something that reached into her soul and took a hold of her.

Oh, she was stupid. Because she'd been warned.

By her father.

By her brother.

By Silas.

And by nearly every woman in the police force.

Rembrandt Stone was an enigma. A charming, handsome, dark haired, blue-eyed enigma, but the kind of man who might drive a woman like her, an investigator born to dig into mysteries until she solved them, crazy.

So she'd walked away. And her phone hadn't rung, not even once.

Which meant that, no, he definitely wasn't obsessed with her.

"He's not watching me," she said now to Silas. "He just wants to make sure I'm—we—are doing our job." She took another picture of the area around the dumpster, behind it, in front of it, then turned and shot the crowd.

It was her crowd shot last time that had helped Rembrandt catch the coffee shop bomber.

"If I'd been better at my job, maybe I would have discovered earlier the connection between Green Earth coffee growers and the social activist group intent on blowing up shops who used their coffee."

Silas looked over at her. "Seriously? The fact that you figured that much out between bombings put you on Chief Booker's radar. Sheesh, Eve, he thinks you're a CSI protege."

She didn't want to tell Silas about the fact it was actually Rembrandt who helped her figure out that connection. Or that she'd talked her kid brother, Asher, into hacking into some database to find the coffee shops who sold the brand.

And while he was busy hacking...

For a delicious, brutal second she was back in the kitchen, her hands on Rembrandt's chest, barely holding on as he kissed her, as she gulped in the taste of him.

She'd made the first move. But she'd been nearly positive, by his reaction, that he was all in. Sometimes she could still feel his hands in her hair, smell the summer air on his skin, the dark, mysterious taste of him and oh brother.

Enough. She had to expunge him from her brain because her father was right. He was trouble. Trouble and adventure and mystery, determination and justice and wow...yes, maybe her father should be worried.

"It was Rem who found the guy. He staked out a coffee shop, driven by one of his legendary hunches, and nearly got killed."

No wonder he wanted to make sure she didn't miss anything. "Rem?"

Eve glanced at Silas, her face growing hot. "Detective Stone."

Silas's mouth pinched. "I don't like him. He's reckless and doesn't care about the rules—"

"He's...driven." And frankly, she knew why.

It's what happened when you lost someone you love. She'd dug up the files on his brother's disappearance. Rembrandt had been twelve, his little brother eight. Yeah, she understood driven. Obsessed.

Motivated. After all she had her own regrets to drive her.

Silas shot her a look. Thin, with hazel-green eyes, he was her best friend from college, the kind of guy who showed up with donuts and coffee to help her cram for her Forensic Toxicology final. Maybe he wanted more—she tried not to notice.

"I think our victim was running. Look here." Silas crouched next to a footprint in the mud near the dumpster. "Look at how deep this print is."

She took a couple shots and moved around for a better view.

"Running from whom?" Rembrandt had come over, and great, how much had he heard? She lowered her camera as he crouched next to the print.

He had nice hands. Solid. Strong.

C'mon, Eve! Focus!

He glanced out across the parking lot, where the police had blocked it off, as if seeing into the past and reconstructing the scene.

His gaze landed on her. "Why does a woman run?"

She didn't want to look at him, but he had these blue eyes. And when he spoke, something terrible and tantalizing rumbled under her skin. "Fear? Hurt?" she managed.

"That's what I was thinking." He still had his gaze on her, looking at her the same way he did this morning.

She always had the sense, except for that moment in the hospital, that Rembrandt Stone could see right through her, into her soul.

Or maybe that's what he did with every woman.

He nodded and got up. "Did you get crowd shots?"

"Yes, she got the crowd shots," Silas said, and his tone sounded like he wanted to add, you moron.

Rem's eyes narrowed.

He seemed to be gritting his jaw as he turned away from Silas, took a breath. "From the direction of the prints, and her body, and even where we found her backpack—about ten feet from her body in the woods—it seems she was running from the road, across the lot. She wasn't at the restaurant—we asked the patrons and no one had seen her, although the owner, Teresa confirmed she's a waitress here. Said she was on shift later this morning. So…maybe she was in a car, about to go in, and got out on the sidewalk and ran instead."

"What tripped her?" Eve said.

Rem pointed to a crack in the driveway, but then shrugged. "Maybe she was tackled."

"You said she had bruises on her neck, as if she might have been strangled?"

"Just a guess," Rem said. "We'll have to wait to get the coroner's report."

"How did she die?" This from Burke, who came up to Rembrandt.

Rembrandt seemed to flinch. "I don't know."

Burke stepped away with his radio.

Eve turned, trying to track the steps Rembrandt had suggested.

"Eve."

She drew in a breath as his voice followed her.

"How are you?"

She peered at him and frowned. "How are you?"

"I'm—oh, you mean the fight this morning?"

He laughed, his blue eyes sparking, and aw, she was such an easy target. "Naw, we were just boxing."

"I meant your wound," she said and tore her gaze away from him before he conjured up more memories than she could deal with. Good thing, really, that it was just a few.

The dangerous few.

"Oh. Yeah. Uh…"

"We haven't talked since the hospital, so—"

"You came to visit me in the hospital?"

"Yes. Don't you remember?" She stared at him, nonplussed.

He made a face. "I was a little…out of it. Not in my right mind, maybe."

Oh. Oh.

Then he wrapped his hand around his neck. "I said something stupid, didn't I?"

"No. You just…you acted like…" Now she was thirteen, her crush declared in front of the entire school.

"I'm an idiot, Eve." He'd dropped his voice, though, glancing over his shoulder. "I'm sorry. I should've reached out."

She blinked at him. Really? The last thing she expected was a self-deprecating apology.

"I've probably been preoccupied with getting back in shape."

Yes. And doing a fine job of it.

Then he smiled, and wow, her world broke right open. No, no, she refused to be this naive again. She wasn't a cop's daughter without knowing when she was being played.

Rembrandt Stone had practically ignored her for an entire month...

"What do you want?" She narrowed an eye.

He frowned, but his smile still sat there. "Nothing, just…"

"What are you doing here?"

The voice stilled her, and she turned as—of course—her father, Inspector Danny Mulligan strode across the parking lot. He wore a dark suit, dress shoes and looked every inch the seasoned investigator from the downtown district.

And, his words clearly weren't for Eve, given the glare he shot Stone's direction.

Rembrandt's mouth opened a second before he closed it and held out his hand.

Her father frowned, but took it. "Stone. I haven't seen you since you...since the bombings. How are you?"

"Back in play." Rembrandt gestured to the yellow-taped crime scene. "Just trying to work the scene before the evidence trail grows cold."

"And if it were on your watch, then maybe that would be a good idea, but your shift doesn't start until, hmm..." He looked at his watch.

Oh, brother. But her father had it out for Rembrandt ever since he wrote the tell-all memoir about his rookie year on the force. The book had landed him on the NYT bestseller list—and on Danny's blacklist.

Cops don't write about their lives, apparently.

But she'd read Rembrandt's book cover to cover, even before she met him. Might have harbored the smallest crush on him—oh, who was she kidding? She'd practically jumped into Rembrandt Stone's arms the moment he looked her way.

Yeah, that wasn't happening again. Ever.

"I just happened to be here," Rembrandt said, and she noticed his voice was easy, as if trying not to get tangled up with Inspector Mulligan's ire.

"Just happened—"

"Dad," Eve said, but he put up his hand.

"Another hunch?"

Rembrandt frowned, glanced at Eve. "No. Just hungry." He

nodded to the diner.

Her father's mouth pinched as he looked at Eve. "Share what you have with our CSI." His gaze went back to Rembrandt. "I'll take it from here."

Rembrandt's jaw tightened. "I got this, Danny. And, I'll tell the parents. I was the one who performed CPR on her."

Her father had turned away, and his back stiffened, but he glanced at Rembrandt and gave a brisk nod before he walked away.

"He doesn't like me," Rembrandt said, his voice sotto.

"He...just...doesn't know you," Eve said.

He sighed. "Yeah."

"So, you think she got out here, at the sidewalk?" Eve had walked over to the edge of the parking lot. "Did anyone from the diner see anything?"

"There's not a clear view to here." Rembrandt was walking along the sidewalk, looking at the windows. "There's too many trees and bushes in the way."

The road was edged by a green space, lilac trees, and flowers in a bed and— "Rem—" Whoops. "Inspector Stone, look." She pointed to a trampling of fallen lilac flowers, smudged into the ground. And in the crushed mess of them, a tread imprint.

She crouched, took a burst of shots.

"Great catch, Eve," Rembrandt said and came over. "That's about two steps from the edge of the road." He walked over to the curb. "She might have gotten out here."

Eve joined him, scanning the other side of the street. The two-lane side street wasn't busy this time of day. The tattoo parlor across the street had just opened, the owner flipping over the paper sign. And next door, through the window of the workout studio, women were holding what looked like a warrior pose.

The air smelled of summer, bacon, and the scent of the lilacs, and she'd bet on a glorious day, with the high in the seventies. Tonight, she'd open the windows and paint her dining room wall.

Maybe talk her brother, Samson, into starting her deck.

"How is your house coming along?" Rembrandt asked.

What, could the man read her mind?

"Good. I'm nearly ready to paint the dining room."

"What color?"

"I don't know yet."

Rembrandt was looking up the street, away from her. "She gets out of a car, here? Or maybe was walking down the sidewalk, although, that's on the other side—"

"What if she ran across the street?"

"From the tattoo parlor?"

"Or...there." She pointed to a clinic the next block down. "What if she was at the women's clinic? It's twenty-four hours."

He was nodding. "Maybe someone picked her up. But why did she get out here?"

"Fear? Hurt?"

He wore an enigmatic expression in his eyes, something almost sad and it stilled her when he said, quietly. "Those are good reasons to run, I guess."

Burke walked over, and Rembrandt turned to him. "We need to talk to someone at that clinic." He pointed down the street.

Burke raised an eyebrow. "Don't tell me."

"It's just—"

"A hunch?"

"Somewhere to start."

Burke glanced at her father. "What about him?"

Inspector Mulligan was talking to Silas.

Rembrandt looked at Eve.

"It's not my job to tell you guys what to do."

The look he gave her was so probing, she should probably run.

She looked away, and down and— "Inspector."

"What?" He crouched next to her as she took a picture, then used her gloves to pick up something bronze and shiny, fallen against the curb of the street.

"I think it's a cuff link." She turned it over. "And, it has a crest on it." She looked up. "Sigma Chi."

"You are simply brilliant, Eve Mulligan." He smiled at her, something so big in his expression, it fell through her, pinning her to the spot.

Everybody was simply, terribly wrong about Rembrandt Stone.

"Rem! Let's go!"

He jerked, as if he came back to himself. "Thanks, Eve. I'll find you later."

I'll find you later.

She watched him go. Yeah, okay. She might like that.

Oh, for Pete's sake. She was pitiful.

She turned back to the crime scene to bag the evidence. Spotted her father looking at her, his jaw tight.

Yeah, well, he wasn't in charge of her life—

And that's exactly what she wanted to say as he came up to her, as she was bagging and labeling the evidence. But the words clogged in her throat.

"Your Mom is hoping you'll stop by for dinner tonight."

"Can't. Have to work late—" She didn't look at him.

"Lucas will be here from Chicago—"

"Dad," she turned to him. "I'll be there this weekend, okay? For the Fourth of July party. I promise."

His mouth tightened, and apparently he just couldn't stop himself from looking over his shoulder, at Rembrandt, then back to her.

"Eve—"

"I know, I know. Rembrandt Stone is trouble." She closed up the bag and put it in another. "There's just something about Rem—Inspector Stone—that just—"

"Stop. He's not a science experiment. And I know you love a good mystery, but stay away from this one. There is something about him that I just don't trust."

"Dad. You don't know him."

"Neither do you. I want you to keep it that way."

She watched him head back to the scene and talk to Silas.

Problem was, she loved a good mystery.

CHAPTER 8

I haven't lost it.

Three years out of the force, and I still know when someone's lying. And right now it's Dr. Lindgren from Planned Parenthood who is trying to tell me she's never seen Gretta Holmes before.

I have to be careful because no one has identified her yet, and the slip of her name might alert Burke the hound dog to keep sniffing around the comment he made as we walked over to the clinic.

C'mon, Rem, how did you know she'd be there?

He said it casually, easy, as if we were continuing a conversation from earlier, and I recognized an interrogation technique that I very nearly fell for.

There are no secrets between Burke and me. Well, there weren't. Apparently now...

"I told you—I heard a scream."

"She was dead, man. Not breathing. What did you hear?" And he's right, of course. I look over at him. An unfamiliar distrust lurks in his eyes. "Don't leave me out in the cold."

"Listen, I don't know where it came from," I say. "Maybe it was one of the pets from the vet clinic next door—don't ferrets scream?"

He's frowning, and what is he going to say—that I'm lying?

"Right," he says and gestures to the green light. But there's a chill in his tone.

He's quiet as I ask about the victim (Gretta) at the front desk, describing her. Yellow pants, long brown hair, jean jacket. Something flickers in the receptionist's eyes, and she's about to answer when Doc Lindgren pops out and intercepts us like she's Vikings cornerback Harrison Smith.

"We can't give out that information without a warrant."

Newsflash—we don't need a warrant to ask for help identifying a victim. And in 1997, the Hippa laws were brand new, many doctors unaware of the rules regarding protected health information. But Lindgren looks a little militant, so I smile and keep my voice friendly. "We are just trying to identify a woman who was murdered just down the street. We believe she visited you today. This is simply an administrative request for help."

"We don't know who you're talking about."

Doc Lindgren is about five six, with crew cut gray hair and the sound and feel of a drill sergeant emanates from her pert little mouth. From the posters on the wall advocating choices and the freedom over your body, I can guess what kind of services they offer.

I've never been political, but my thoughts about abortion sure swung toward life after Ashley was born.

"Are you sure?" Burke asks. "We think she might have come here for help."

"We don't turn anyone away, if that's what you're insinuating." Her mouth collects spittle along the edges, as if we have her worried.

"What about—" Burke starts, and I'm not sure what he's

going to ask, but Lindgren cuts him off.

"No. No one like that was here."

The overweight woman at the front desk has chewed her fingernails to the nub. She looks about twenty years old and keeps glancing at the door.

"Our request is not against the law," I add. And, it's not. "I can have my office send you a written request—"

"You need to leave."

"Listen." I tenor my voice to the sotto voce I use when talking to an angry Eve. "What if it were your daughter, strangled and bleeding on the street, and no one knew it? She could go for years without being identified—" And this isn't actually true because after a modicum of searching, we'll identify her as a runaway in our system, reported less than three months ago, but Gretta's connection to the clinic is a new clue, and maybe we're one step closer to whoever put their hands around her neck. "And we're just asking for help to put her mother's mind at rest. To keep her daughter from being buried in an unmarked grave. Years of grief not knowing…"

Lindgren's jaw tightens.

Out of the corner of my eye, and behind the doctor, the receptionist is scribbling on a piece of paper.

"You do know that an autopsy will uncover anything medical we need to know," Burke says. "And we can get a warrant—"

"Do that," Lindgren snaps and turns away.

Burke blows out a breath.

But I take the piece of paper that the receptionist—named Grace by the tag on her shirt, which feels appropriate, by the way—gives me.

Thank you, I mouth and go outside. Hand the paper to Burke.

"Gretta Holmes," he says.

85

Bingo, but that will save us time. And time is the ticket when solving a case like this.

We walk back to my Camaro.

"You nearly had me crying in there," Burke says. He looks at me. "Thinking about your brother?"

Yeah, maybe on some level. It's always there, never buried deep enough to fully let go of. My kid brother who vanished while we were out riding our bikes. My mother never quite recovered, and our family fell apart in the waiting years. According to the history I know, some fishermen snagged his body while out fishing for walleye in a lake near our home just a month ago.

But no. I was thinking of Ashley. I nod, however.

"How are your parents?" Burke asks, and I should know the answer, but I haven't a clue.

In the previous timeline, my mother had a stroke the day she received the long-awaited news.

In this timeline, or at least the one I just left, I remember seeing a picture of them with a parrot and an umbrella drink on a recent cruise, so maybe that went better the second time around. So, "As well as can be expected."

Burke says nothing and we get into the Camaro and pull out. He'd left his boring Integra at the gym, and we drive back to Carefree Highway, an ironic ballad by Gordon Lightfoot, about picking up pieces of shattered dreams.

Eve is back in my head, my mind circling around her smile, her red hair flinging out of the ponytail she'd shoved it into after the gym, looking at me with those hazel-green eyes, and—

"You think she was pregnant?" Burke asks, turning down the radio. I hate when he does that. Feels like a man should be able to control his own volume.

"Dunno." I can't remember from the autopsy, but it seems

that would have stuck with me. "Maybe she had an STD test."

"Working girl?"

I can't remember, but I hope not. "She didn't look like it."

"She might be in the system."

Most definitely, but I don't want to sound too eager, so I nod. "Good idea."

As if fate has my number, Loggins and Messina come on with Danny's Song, and I hum along.

"You like her."

I glance at Burke and he's grinning, his dark eyes shiny.

"Who?" I say, and my voice is too high.

Burke laughs and shakes his head. "Aw, you like trouble too much, Rem. I told you to stay away from her. She's a blue blood. Imagine what Danny Mulligan would do to you if you two got involved."

Already done, buddy. Involved with a capital I. But I do make a face because I hated the idea that Danny never liked me.

I'll fix that, too.

I'm not much of a praying man, but sometimes, like now, I'd like to see what I have to barter.

"I thought you were over her."

"What gave you that idea?" And now I've given myself away, Burke the slick one.

"Just…I don't know. After the bombings, after the stabbing, she came to the hospital and sat by your bedside. And when you woke up, you barely grunted her direction."

Oh, I could strangle young me. Apparently, my idiocy started early.

"I was just…I wanted to get back to work."

"And today? What was that?"

"She looked good, didn't she?"

He cocks his head at me. "Did you hear nothing of what I just said? Inspector Mulligan has your number. You even get near her, he'll send the entire First after you—"

"Calm down, Burke. By the time the weekend's over, Danny Mulligan's going to love me."

Burke raises an eyebrow. "Really?"

"Yep." I turn into Quincy's and pull up to his Integra. "You just wait." And then I wink.

I don't know what's wrong with me. Maybe it's the fact that I feel a little bit invincible, the wind under me.

I can change time.

Okay, and yeah, I very much remember the mess I made of things in the future. But I'm going to find a version, a timeline re-write where eighteen-year-old girls don't get strangled in alleyways, where fathers and sons aren't gunned down in the street, where little girls aren't abducted from their beds at night.

And yes, you're saying, the world is full of tragedy and violent crimes and you can't save everyone, Batman, but this is my time-line, er, timelines and I can fix what I want, so leave me alone.

This is going to end well.

Redbone confirms it with Come and Get Your Love as I pull into the precinct station. We're still hanging out at the 5th precinct while the downtown office finishes up the remodel. This office on Nicollet is new and shiny and nothing of the exhausted facade of future days. I get out, and saunter into the station, humming.

I enter, and for a second, I'm thrown.

What? My office isn't in the middle of the conference room command center, but parked in the corner, the farthest from the coffee machine as if Booker has it in for me.

Burke's office, I might add is the closest, so I guess we all know why he became Deputy Chief. But I'll sort that out when I get back.

I fill a coffee cup as I walk by the machine and am just setting it on my desk—predictably piled high with file folders—next to a chunky box monitor (and I'm trying not to laugh) when I hear a voice.

"Rem. My office. Now."

Chief John Booker. And I don't know why but every time I hear his voice tunneling through the past to grab me, it takes a piece out of me.

After my Mikey died, Booker started coming around, updating the family on the case. He always had time for me. He was my mentor until we had the fight of the century the day I quit the force. Up till that moment I considered him a father.

Now, he's standing in the door of his office, a hand on the frame and I have the sense of being summoned to the principal's office, the tiny hairs rising on the back of my neck.

Booker wears every case—especially the few unsolved ones—in every craggy line on his face. Short clipped graying hair, he has the dry humor and few words persona of a Montana cowboy. Think a towering, solemn version of Sheriff Dillon, from Gunsmoke. A couple people look up as I walk by, a smattering of pity in their eyes.

They don't realize that although Booker has a look that can stop a man from drawing a piece, he's also the guy who actually gives someone the time of day and isn't afraid to wait for you to speak.

He closes the door behind him and hangs on the knob for a bit.

Gestures toward a chair with his chin.

So this is a sitting talk. Great.

I lower myself into the chair, not sure what I did. I'm flying blind here, now on both sides of the timeline, and I'm just hoping that my respect for Booker in my youth was enough to keep me from doing something colossally stupid.

"How long?" His voice is soft, but there's steel in the question. He folds his arms over his chest and walks to his desk, leaning on the front edge.

"How…what?"

He draws in a breath. "I started to suspect something during the bombings. You just…" He shakes his head. "Rem, there's no way you followed the hunch in your gut to that third location."

Remember, I was undercover for a while. So, I angle him a look. "What are you talking about? Eve and I made the connection between the coffee suppliers—"

Booker cuts me off with a compound word I've rarely heard him say.

Okay.

"How long?"

I'm still not following, although a slow creep in the center of my gut is telling me—

"You have it, don't you?"

"What?"

He stares at me for a full ten seconds before answering. "My watch."

I look down at my wrist. Swallow.

"How long have I been dead?"

I stare at him, my eyes wide, blown apart. "I—"

"Did you give me a good eulogy?" He grins and I'm frozen. Because what am I going to do? Confess that I'm from the future? See, even to me it sounds crazy, and I'm living it.

He holds up his hand. "Okay. I get it. You don't want to tell me. And probably that's right, because I shouldn't know."

Now, I want to tell him. Please, don't track down Leo Fitzgerald at his house. Don't go inside. You'll set off a trigger line and…

"How'd you know?"

"You kidding?" He grunts and chuckles at the same time. "It's written all over your face in block letters."

I sigh. "I have questions—"

Booker holds up his hand again. "In time. I'm going to tell you only what you need to know, what Chief of Police Greg Sulzbach said to me when he gave me the watch."

My eyes widen because I remember him. He died of cancer a few years before I joined the force.

"I looked just as wild-eyed when I realized that…well, that I could go back and get justice." He raises his eyebrows and I nod, my first acquiesce to the truth.

But, Booker knows. He knows, and maybe, suddenly, I have an ally.

"I have to tell you something, Chief—"

"No, you don't."

"But—"

"Here are the rules. The biggest one, the one that is never, ever to be broken…Don't change the past."

Oh.

"You don't know what else you could change, and what chaos you could cause."

I look away, my mouth pursed, because I could have used this conversation, well, a couple days, one month and twenty-plus years ago.

Before I overwrote my life.

But really, I couldn't let people just…die, right?

He gave the watch to the wrong person if he expected me not to get involved.

"The watch was created to find answers, bring closure. To solve cases. And keep people from suffering."

Now I understand. Booker gave me the watch because, out of all his detectives, I had an upfront and center view of suffering, thanks to my brother.

And here I thought he believed in me.

"The watch can only take you back to the moment a crime has been committed. And you have forty-eight hours to solve it."

"What if I don't solve it?"

He sighs. "Then it never gets solved." His mouth pinches. "Try not to let that happen."

Yeah, baby, I knew it. I mean, at this point, we all knew Booker could go back in time also, but remember, I guessed it back at the Foxes'. Some sort of smug satisfaction shows on my face, because Booker frowns at me.

"What?" he asks.

"That's why you have such an amazing record of closed cases. Because you went back in time and solved them. That is cheating."

He cocks his head, narrows one eye.

I am still grinning at him.

"Fine. You're right, kid. But it was never about the record. It was about justice."

Right. Yes. Justice.

And maybe Eve. And fixing the wounds of our past.

"Listen, if you have the watch, you also have your cold cases. Solve them. Methodically. One by one. Don't skip any. And by the way, you can only solve your cold cases—no one else's. And don't ever forget that you have people's lives, their futures, in your hands."

That's a little heavy, but my mind goes to Art, and I can't shake the idea that something I did landed him in that chair. I feel a little like I did when I took my oath of honor. On my honor, I will never betray my badge, my integrity, my character or the public trust.

Oh, man.

But what if… "Chief. I know about a shooting—"

"Don't—"

"But it's someone—"

"Do you know who killed him?"

"Yes."

"Then your job is done."

"He's not dead yet!"

"For you, he is."

"But he's…he's a cop."

Booker freezes, and he's shut down, his mouth a grim line.

"Book. Please. Just this once." And okay, twice, because, you know, Ashley. But by then, maybe I'll have rewritten time, and Booker and I might not have had this conversation. Or maybe we will have and…

I'm seriously confused. But we all know that there are some promises we can't keep, some rules that must be broken, right?

He swallows. Then looks at me and shakes his head. "No, Rem. You don't understand. You can't win against time. You aren't here to save people. Changing history…you don't know what you're messing with. You don't know that the tiniest change could, well it could destroy lives."

I feel like he's seeing inside my soul to my sins. I tighten my jaw, try and keep an even stare. Me? Change history?

His mouth tightens. "This…gift…is to help give people closure. To let them live in peace. Nothing more. Just solve the crime for which you're here and leave the rest to history."

One could argue…

But that's enough of a gray statement for me to nod, without guile.

"Good." And then he smiles, something warm in his eyes. "I knew I could trust my gut on you." He clamps me on the shoulder. "I do hope we ended well."

We will. I vow it in my soul.

CHAPTER 9

Gretta Holmes deserved justice, and with every bone in her body, Eve would find it for her.

Even if she starved to death doing it.

While Silas categorized all the items taken from the crime scene, Eve had gone down to the Hennepin County Medical Center to pull fresh evidence and take pictures before Gretta's body was sent to the Office of the Medical Examiner. Silas had already left for lunch by the time Eve returned from the morgue.

Now, she stood in front of the cork board in her lab, studying the array of photographs. The sun cast bare shadows through the window of her downtown office, across the stainless steel counter tops, her workstation, a cold cup of coffee, and the collected crime scene evidence, categorized by Silas. Backstreet Boys crooned As Long As You Love Me from a boom box shoved beneath her metal desk.

Her stomach growled, but she ignored it.

Knowing the victim by name only deepened the tragedy and urge for justice that burrowed inside Eve. She'd dissected plenty of crime scenes since joining Booker's precinct a month ago, but for some reason, this crime latched onto a place deep inside.

Gretta was young, and the parallel scars on her arm bespoke a profound pain that triggered a memory Eve didn't want to revisit.

She'd been a teenager, too, once upon a time, who didn't know where to put her grief, her loss, her guilt. Who turned it inward to her body and left a few self-inflicted scars.

She wasn't that troubled teenager anymore—long from it—but seeing the scars on Gretta's arms galvanized Eve.

Who hurt you?

Stone was a good detective to have identified Gretta so quickly. But Eve already knew that—after all, he'd tracked down the third coffee shop bomber with only fragments of clues.

She should have been with him, helping him.

Eve turned away from the pictures and headed out to the hallway toward the vending machine.

This time, she had every intent of solving this case, or at least helping, before Rembrandt walked into an ambush with a knife-wielding bomber.

She stood in front of the vending machine, perusing her choices, and settled on a Diet Coke and a Snickers bar.

Why does a woman run?

Rembrandt's voice clung to her, and it felt more like a real question than rhetorical, because of course he'd know. Like she said. Fear. Hurt.

Gretta probably fled from both. She'd skinned her knees and her hands, so maybe she'd actually fallen from the car. A button had popped off her jacket, as if it had been grabbed. Maybe to stop her? Eve hadn't found a button at the scene, but it might be worth a return visit.

Fingerprints pressed Gretta's throat in three perfectly formed bruises. Eve had tried to lift prints from her skin, but it was too rigid and oily.

The only other possession, besides her clothing, was a twenty dollar bill Rembrandt had found stuck in her grip. She'd tried to find prints off it too, but she couldn't find anything clear. Money usually passed too many hands to be conclusive.

"Oh, so we're there are we?"

She turned and hated her stupid heart for its wild thump when Inspector Stone sauntered into her office. He'd clearly been driving with the window down because his dark hair was wild, and he wore a hint of the summer sun on his skin under his open collar and face.

Shoot, he was handsome and down, girl.

Except, he had recently called her brilliant, hello.

"What? Where are we?"

He set a bag down on the counter and gestured to the candy bar. "Put down the chocolate, Eve." He reached out to ease it from her hand. Wrapped it up. "I brought you a sandwich. It's from the Dayton Deli. Ham salad, on whole wheat."

He brought her lunch? "I love ham salad," Eve said, opening the bag. She glanced at him. "Have you been talking to Silas?"

He ran a zipper across his lips and gave her another of those cryptic smiles and oh, her father was dead on.

Rembrandt Stone was a mystery she intended to solve.

He walked over to her wall and stared at it. "What happened to you, Gretta?"

He went very quiet then, as if waiting for an answer, and Eve didn't know what to say.

Finally, he said, "I called her parents. I'm going to meet them at the County Medical Examiner's office."

"Do they know yet?"

"I told them we had an update on their daughter's case."

"Oh, Rem. You should have gone over to their house and told them personally."

She didn't even realize she'd said the words until he turned, his eyes wide. "Really?"

She nodded, and made a face, and not just because of her comment, but, Rem? Really? Although, he'd told her to call him Rem, once upon a time. And he hadn't just corrected her, so...

He blew out a breath. "You're right. I'll remember that."

She pulled out the sandwich and broke off half. Joined Rembrandt at the board.

"So, what do you know?"

"She has abrasions on her hands and knees, and strangulation marks on her neck, but we'll wait for the M.E.'s report on any trace evidence on her body."

Oh, the tangy pickles and mayo of the ham sandwich went right to her bones and soothed the savage beast inside. She might have even uttered a small sound of appreciation.

He looked down at her and grinned, his blue eyes shiny.

She swallowed past the sudden lump in her throat.

He turned to the evidence table. "Is this the contents from her purse?"

"Yes. Silas found everything from lipstick to a hairbrush to a wallet, but no driver's license. She looks about eighteen, however, so maybe she never got one."

"What's this?" Rem had picked up a plastic bag with a credit card inside.

"It was in her wallet."

"Robert D. Swenson."

"Silas is running a stolen card check on the number."

He set down the card. "We ran a check on Gretta. She's been missing for three months, according to a report filed by her parents."

"So, a runaway." Eve debated, then, "She had old scars on her arms—cutting."

Rembrandt's face twisted. "Really? Self harm?"

She nodded.

His gaze flickered down to an old—very old—scar on her arm. One she had truly forgotten about until today.

She had the weirdest urge to cover her arm with her hand, but it was already covered by her shirt, so...

He couldn't possibly know.

"Yes. So maybe that was why she ran away."

"It's usually caused by a very deep pain," he said quietly, and met her eyes. "One the victim doesn't know how to carry. Sometimes, they hurt themselves on the outside to match the pain on the inside."

Huh.

"I can't imagine how much pain someone has to be in to hurt themselves." He wore so much compassion in his expression, she had to look away. "No pain is worth that."

She didn't know why she had the sense he might be talking to her. But, "Yeah, I know."

Oh, she didn't know why she'd said that, either. But after a moment, "She lost a button on her jacket."

That sounded lame.

"Really?" Rem said, as if it might be vital information, although maybe he'd just sensed, suddenly, the way too intimate conversation. He looked back at the pictures. "Have you ever recently, uh, seen any more victims with this same...well with a twenty dollar bill in their hand?" He was staring at the picture of the bill, extracted at the hospital, but with the crime scene evidence.

"No. Why?"

"It's just strange, don't you think?"

"Maybe the guy she ran from was a John, and he was paying her."

"I don't think so. I think Gretta was pregnant."

"Why do you think that?" She finished off the first half of her sandwich.

"Look at the contents of her bag. Where are her tampons? I don't know a woman alive at this age who doesn't have tampons."

Huh. "Right."

"And that clinic was an abortion clinic."

Oh. "Did you talk to the M.E. yet?"

"No. And I'm not going to ask if she was pregnant in front of her parents."

"The M.E. said the strangulation marks looked old, at least by a day. What if the guy in the car was the father of her child? Maybe she told him she didn't want an abortion, and they got in a fight."

"And she got out and ran and slipped..."

Pregnant. "How awful. To lose a child—and a grandchild. Her parents will be devastated."

Rem took a breath. Nodded.

"I don't know how you get over losing a child. I mean, no one is supposed to outlive their children..."

Beside her, Rembrandt had drawn in a breath, held it.

She wanted to give herself a smack. "Oh, Rem, I'm sorry. I didn't even think..."

He looked at her, stricken, his eyes wide. Then, he blinked. "Oh, you mean my brother."

Who did he think she meant?

"Yeah. My parents struggled for a very long time. It nearly took them apart."

"I don't know how they survived."

"I think you'd have to hold onto each other. Otherwise, what else do you have?" He seemed to be looking clear through her when he spoke, as if he could impart some wisdom to her soul.

Her voice turned small under the weight of it. "Yeah."

He looked away, blinking, and oh, why had she brought up his brother? Almost, without thinking, she touched his arm. "I'm so sorry, Rem, for your loss."

When he looked at her again, his eyes had reddened.

And there he was, the man she'd met a month ago, before the stabbing. Shelby could just shut up about Rembrandt and his toughened heart. The man was sweet and considerate and...

Had she learned nothing over the last few brutally quiet weeks? A smile, a ham sandwich and a little flattery and she was ready to throw herself into his arms?

Please. She turned away and picked up the cuff link. "Sigma Chi."

"I think that's a fraternity at the University of Minnesota." His voice sounded a little funny, but she didn't comment.

"I'll see if I can track down when these were cast."

"Thanks, Eve. I knew I could count on you."

Oh boy. She glanced at the sandwich bag. "Thanks for the grub."

"Yeah, it's easy to get focused on a case, right?"

He said it like he knew what it felt like to have a case burrow in your mind and never leave, itch you with questions until they were answered. "Yeah, it is."

"You have to learn to take breaks, let your mind think. You get so focused on something it can keep you pinned to it, and then it will derail your entire life. And your life has to be bigger than the work, the questions, the frustration, right?"

She nodded, but, "Don't you get obsessed? I mean...there's this reputation—"

He put up his hand. "That was the old me. The new me knows how to let go, get some perspective, and how to keep the questions from taking over my life."

She supposed a life-threatening injury might do that.

His phone buzzed and he pulled it off his belt. "I gotta go, but...um. I was thinking. You might want to try Powell Bluff."

She had nothing. "What?"

"It's a paint color. Sort of a beige. I think you'll like it. For your dining room."

"Oh. Okay..."

He was heading toward the door.

"Rembrandt?"

He turned. And for the life of her, she didn't know why the words simply formed and bubbled out of her, as if she had unstopped a geyser, but, "We're having a party on Saturday night. A Fourth of July gig with my family. On the lake. Would you like to join us?"

He stood there in the silhouette of the doorway, dressed in his suit, tall and wide-shouldered, powerful, shadowed, something about him both familiar and yet deliciously mysterious and a smile crept up his face, chasing all her doubts from her brain. "I wouldn't miss it for the world."

She turned back to the boards, no longer hungry.

CHAPTER 10

I know I shouldn't get cocky, but things are looking up, don't you think?

Eve still likes me. Even if I did blow it a month ago, today, I made her smile. I know the ham salad sandwich was cheating, but hey, give me a break, I'm a desperate man.

I only have one chance to get this right.

So, yes, I scrolled through my twenty-plus-year-old knowledge of my Eve, and remembered how she forgot to eat when she focused too long on a case. In fact, she's always been just as obsessed as I am, which we're going to fix right now.

Then again, it was my obsessiveness and fear of losing myself and my family that led me to the Colossal Argument between me and Booker.

So, maybe I just saved us all from future heartache.

I'm feeling fairly stalwart—thinking of the inscription on my watch—as I head outside into the parking lot, get into the Camaro and motor down to 305 Chicago Avenue, to the Medical Examiner's office. It's located in the basement of the old HCMC medical building. It'll move in about a decade to the western suburbs, a shiny new building with all the latest technology. But now it's just a few blocks away. I turn up the volume to Don't Look Back, by Boston, a stalwart song if ever there was one.

There are only four cars in the lot—a Lexus, the coroner's van, and an Integra. Burke has beaten me here and I spot him standing in the shade near the door. The July heat hasn't wilted his shirt, and of course he's wearing his suit coat.

I've ditched my tie, my jacket, and rolled up my sleeves.

I shut my door. "What?"

"You went to see Eve, didn't you?" He gives me his raised eyebrows look.

I grin and he rolls his eyes, even as he leans off his car and falls in step with me. "You know you're playing with fire."

"I'm not scared of Danny Mulligan."

"You should be, Rem. He's not in charge of the Gang Activities unit for no reason. He's the kind of guy who knows every hoodlum in downtown Minneapolis on a first name basis—because he's tracked them down and arrested them. If he finds out you're sniffing around Eve, you're going to start getting visits—"

I hold up my hand. "He's going to like me. You just wait and see." I reach for the door handle. "Besides, Eve is worth it."

Burke purses his lips and follows me in.

The place is clean, clinical, and our footsteps echo off the tile floor as we head down the hallway to the tiny waiting room, more of an alcove with chairs that line the walls.

I jerk at the sight of Jeff and Karen Holmes. They look exactly the same as I remember them, and of course they would because they, um, are the same. Jeff is dressed in a blue suit, yellow tie, a white oxford, and glances at his watch as if he might be annoyed. Again, I don't like him. Karen, however, looks at me with a terrible mix of hope and dread in her eyes. She's wearing a pink summer sweater, a pair of white jeans and dockers, her hair straight and when she tucks it behind her ear, I realize...

I don't want to do this again.

It was hard enough the first time, with Karen collapsing onto the floor, her husband stalking down the hallway to leave her behind and Burke and I calling 9-1-1.

I hope Burke has his phone out and I instinctively step closer to Karen before I stick out my hand to Jeff and introduce myself. His grip is cool, quick and firm like we might be here to make a deal. Buying a car or something. I've forgotten what the man does for a living, but something about him still raises my skin.

"I'm so sorry to have to call you in—" Burke begins.

"Have you found her?" Karen touches my arm, swallows.

I touch her hand, removing it from my arm. "Yes, but..." I glance at the chairs. "Maybe we should sit."

She presses her hands to her mouth and I manage to get her to the chairs before she goes white. "Is she..."

Burke takes a deep breath. "I'm so sorry, ma'am but, yes. We found your daughter this morning."

This time I have something to add. "We tried to revive her, but despite all our efforts..." Now it's my turn to breathe deep. "I'm sorry, but she didn't make it."

She leans over, her hands around her waist, and begins to keen.

Jeff's face has hardened, and he looks away.

Well, at least we aren't calling 9-1-1 again.

"I'm so sorry for your loss," Burke says.

"Are you sure it's her?" Karen has gulped back her horror, her voice cut to a whisper. She's reached out for my hand, and somehow found it.

If she goes down, I got her.

"That's why we asked you here," I say, and glance at Jeff. "We need a positive I.D."

"I'll do it," Jeff says quickly, and gets up.

"I want to see her!" Karen bounces to her feet. "I want to see her, Jeff." She has her hands pressed to her mouth, her breaths hiccupping.

I'm not sure about the wisdom of his agreement, so we follow them down the hall and I knock on the door.

The Medical Examiner, a man by the name of Kirchner is waiting for us and opens the door to allow them in. He introduces himself.

This part is new. Last time, neither parent identified her until after Karen visited the ER, and then, only Jeff confirmed his daughter's identity.

Now, I'm glancing at Burke, staying close to Karen.

They approach a sheet-draped body on a gurney, and I easily remember Gretta on the pavement, pale, not breathing, her makeup smudged, as if she'd been crying. Funny that thought comes to mind. Crying, as if she'd been in a fight.

With the father of her child? I won't ask the M.E. if he's determined if she was pregnant. Not yet.

But it's on my radar.

That and the cufflink Eve found. Last time we hadn't been at the scene at the same time, didn't talk, she didn't find the cufflink and the clinic didn't register on my radar.

I'm sure a thousand other tiny changes have already occurred, but it's too late to stop them.

Sorry, Booker.

At least Gretta hasn't been transferred yet to a body bag. The smell of formaldehyde and other preservatives sour the air, bouncing off the stainless-steel surfaces, the bone hard cement floor.

Jeff is still as he stands beside the body. I find it odd that Karen doesn't reach for his hand.

Kirchner warns them, then pulls back the sheet.

Suddenly, I'm not watching them grieve over the body of their eighteen-year-old daughter. Instead, I'm in an updated version of this room, Eve's hand in mine as we stare in horror at Ashley's bruised body. Maybe it's my recollection of the picture I saw in Booker's file or…or maybe it's an actual memory. But I can see her hair, muddied and wrenched free of her braids, her tiny lips, pale in death. I want to take her hand, run my thumb over it, urge her back to life.

Daddy's here, honey.

My breath catches and, Oh, God, it feels like an actual memory, with the punch right in the middle of my sternum, every cell in my body wanting to scream at the swollen, battered visage of my beautiful daughter. Eve's hand is in mine, tightening, then she utters a sound, not a scream, more of a rending of her spirit, her heart. A tearing from the fabric of her soul.

No wonder I lost us.

It. Was. Real.

It is a terrible, brutal, soul carving horror to imagine—experience—your own child's death. The room begins to spin.

I haven't rewritten anything, not yet, and a poison fills my body, every pore, every cell as I blink hard, trying to wipe the image away.

Acid lines my throat.

My daughter died, and I suddenly remember everything. The rank smell of the forest on her body, the cruel face of death, the way Kirchner—yes, still the same man, older, silent—waited for us to nod.

Yes. This is Ashley.

Yes, our daughter.

Yes, the very life of us…

I too want to drop to the ground.

"No," Karen says now, and her horror is merciful as it yanks me from the memory.

She puts her hand to her mouth. "No—"

And then, she turns and collapses into my arms.

I'm right there to catch her, as if on instinct. Muscle memory kicking in.

She is weeping, hysterical and not surprisingly, her husband turns and walks from the room.

So maybe you can't exactly change history.

I shake my head. No. I refuse to believe that.

I lower Karen Holmes to the floor, sinking with her. What else am I going to do? I understand. My heart, my soul, understands.

So I hold her, a little awkwardly, maybe, and Burke is giving me a look, but it's all I have right now.

For both of us.

She weeps and I tighten my grip.

I'm not crying. But my jaw is tight just in case.

Kirchner pulls the sheet back over Gretta's body.

"We need to ask a few questions," Burke starts but I shake my head, then nod toward the door. Go after Jeff.

He reads my mind, as usual and heads outside.

Kirchner melds into the wall somewhere, and the room is quiet, save for Karen Holmes's sobbing.

Her hand fists my shirt, turning it black with her mascara and now I remember why I don't wear suits. But it's okay. It's the least I can do.

Except, I'm going to do more, much more. "I'm so sorry."

She finally leans away and stares at me, not really seeing me. "We called the police and no one did anything about it. They said she was a runaway, and that she was old enough to leave home, but…" Her jaw trembles.

Parents know, right? When something is wrong?

She finally meets my eyes. "I don't remember your name."

"Rembrandt. Inspector Rembrandt Stone."

She is trying to gather herself, searching her pockets and I remember I still carry a handkerchief, so I hand it to her.

The action feels so familiar, I'm digging through my layers to find the memory, and latch onto a different one.

Eve. She's sitting in the waiting room of a hospital, on brown chairs, her hands over her head, bent over with the news of Danny's death. It's so clear, I can hear her sobbing even as I crouch in front of her, hand her my handkerchief and take her into my arms.

It's the day I knew, right to my core, that my heart would belong to her. If only I'd spent a little more time listening to that voice instead of my ambition back then. But the memory is swift and thorough and is just as real as Ashley's death.

Eve will still lose her father and her brother, and then her beloved daughter.

I haven't changed history. I've just given it a shove in the wrong direction.

Tonight, I intend to knock it on its backside and drag it kicking and screaming back into place.

I help Karen off the floor and out into the foyer where Burke is interviewing Jeff.

Glance at the clock.

I have roughly six hours to track down Danny's stakeout… and keep him from committing the act that will destroy us all.

CHAPTER 11

Jeff and Karen Holmes give us nothing new, at least from my recollection.

Gretta Holmes turned eighteen three months ago, and after a blistering fight with her father about her boyfriend, she ran away from home. They reported her missing, but the police never followed up because of the nature of her disappearance.

Besides, the parents suspected she was holed up with friends from school. Periodically, Karen had received phone calls from Gretta and had even given her money through a trusted friend, her softball coach.

Burke is giving me a run-down of this familiar information as we stand outside in the parking lot of a McDonald's in Uptown. The sun is heavy on the backside of the day, and the heat is starting to run down my back. Burke is eating an ice cream cone. I'm finishing off a Diet Coke.

I know what's going to happen next, also. Burke and I will interview Teresa, the manager at Lulu's diner, and she'll tell us about how Gretta worked as a waitress. How she was a favorite with the patrons, and especially one who came in often. A blonde man, a little thick around the middle, who Gretta occasionally joined for an after-shift milkshake. Mid-thirties, he sometimes wore a suit, other times a t-shirt and jeans.

It rolls through my mind now, that maybe this guy is the father of her baby.

However, in the past, and probably again, Teresa hadn't seen him on the day of Gretta's murder—today—and Gretta was scheduled to work.

"I think we should head to the diner, and talk to her boss, again," Burke says, predictably. "She was busy with the morning rush when we were there. I'm thinking she'll have more information for us. Maybe she saw the car that picked her up."

The car.

Yes, she had seen a car because it was remarkably out of place. A Lexus ES. Good memory jog, Burke.

But I just hum, and nod because circling through my brain is also the little information I know about Danny's murder.

Danny and Asher were at a convenience store just down the road from their home, picking up ice cream when the shooting occurred. They'd just gotten out of Danny's truck, were walking into the building when a 1990 Buick wood-paneled station wagon pulled into the lot, and someone pulled out an AR-15 semi-automatic rifle and peppered the Mulligan men with bullets.

No one else was injured.

Danny and Asher died on the spot, the wagon drove away and Booker asked for my help on the case twenty-four hours after I'd held Eve in my arms at the hospital.

My guess is that he knew I needed something—anything—to do.

Now, I wonder if Booker had other motives, even then. Like...if we never found the murderers, maybe I could circle back in time…

The thought has my brain in knots, but I look up when Burke says, "Did you think the father was acting weird?"

"Yeah." I pause. "I don't know. Maybe he couldn't look at his daughter like that. Beaten, dead, knowing that he wasn't there to stop it."

Burke finishes off his cone. "He looked angry. Like he'd like to end somebody."

"Wouldn't you, if your daughter was murdered?" That came out a little too strong, so I add a shrug. "I'm just guessing."

Burke nods, wiping his hands. "But that's what we're here for. So he doesn't do something stupid."

Like turn into a drunk and destroy the only thing he has left, his marriage? I suddenly wonder where Burke's been over the past two years as I tried to put together the pieces of my life. "Maybe he doesn't trust us to find the killer. Maybe he feels like he's alone in the fight, and that everyone has given up. That if he doesn't do something, then no one will."

I must be channeling the future me because there is too much passion in my voice to not let it take root and find hollow places.

"All I know is that if anything ever happened to my child, I'd never stop looking for the killer."

I meet Burke's gaze, something of defiance in it.

He frowns. "Neither would I."

I feel like there's a promise embedded in there, and I nod.

A smile curves into Burke's face. "There you are. Finally."

Huh?

"After you got stabbed, you sort of, I don't know, walked out of your life for a while. As if you'd been sidelined. You seemed to be phoning it in, and I started to wonder if we were still in this together." Burke slaps my shoulder. "Maybe you have a chance with

Eve after all."

"Of course I do," I say, but his words have found a place inside that unnerves me.

What happens to me, the other me, when I leave?

By going back in time, rewriting my consciousness, am I turning my gray matter to pulp?

I get in the car and follow Burke back to the station. The hour is late, and I need more information on the stakeout and events of tonight's shooting.

The shooting that leads to the drive-by gang response.

I remember this case better, of course. Danny had been the head of a drug-related, gang-centered task force. After his murder, I did a search on the Buick station wagon and unearthed roughly four thousand hits. I turned to my network of informants and hit a dead end.

Not a whisper of who had put out a hit on Danny and Asher.

Over the years, I'd fielded false leads, and a few informants who wanted to trade, but nothing unearthed solid evidence on who had shot them.

But I knew who was behind it.

Like Eve said, it's Hassan Abdilhali, a Somalian warlord who's applied his skills to the disenfranchised, disparate refugee population. How do I know?

Because his brother's death, on this night, makes tomorrow's headlines.

I just can't remember where it goes down.

I'm desperate for something to jog my memory as we pull up to Lulu's. Burke goes in, and I follow him, my stomach stopping to beg as the smell of greasy french fries hits me. The place is decorated fresh out of the fifties, with metal stools at the malt counter, and red vinyl booths lined up along the side of the joint.

Elvis is singing All Shook Up on the jukebox in the corner, and the menu board matches the waitress's pink dresses. A malt machine fires up, and my stomach whines.

I should have had an ice cream cone.

Burke slides onto a stool and asks to see Teresa.

She'll ignore him, mostly, and talk to me, standing a little too close, touching my arm, so this time I'll let Burke do the talking.

In the meantime, I wander over to the rack and pick up the newspaper. Paging through the police beat in the back, I scan for recent arrests.

I hear laughter and Teresa is standing close to Burke now. Touching his arm.

Sorry pal. I turn back to the paper, and an article in the back, page twelve, catches my eye.

Two young men had been arrested in north Minneapolis for petty theft. They had mug shots. And yes, I'm profiling, but they look Somalian. I read the names.

Jamal Gabeyre and Ari Kamas.

What if they weren't just thugs, but small-time dealers? And what if they could lead me to the bigger operation?

My gut says that Danny has already figured this out.

I close the paper and shove it back in the rack.

Burke is finishing up, Teresa gesturing with her hands. "And then the Lexus just drove away, about twenty minutes before you all showed up."

"And Gretta was how late for work?"

"She wasn't. She usually came early. I didn't expect her for another half hour." Now, her gaze lands on me. She's applied fresh red lipstick, but it doesn't help.

"And you didn't see Gretta get in the car?"

"No. It was parked against the curb, but I'm sure I would have seen someone get out of a Lexus…"

I turn around and look at the view through the front. "Not from here."

"No, in the kitchen, there's a back door. And my office window faces the street."

My guess is that her testimony might be easily swiss-cheesed under cross-examination, but I don't push it. No need for hostility here. But I file the information away.

"Do you remember seeing any other cars?"

She lifts a shoulder. "Not really. I wasn't looking. Nothing out of the ordinary. Maybe a caravan, or a couple sedans. The usual crowd."

"And the man she is often here with…what can you tell us about him?"

"Seemed nice. Not a boyfriend, but someone who cared. He paid for her meal, sometimes. He drove a nice car—a corvette."

I don't remember that from before. This is where I pull from Eve's information. Credit card man. "Robert Swenson?"

"I don't know." She makes a face. "But…oh, maybe. She called him Rob sometimes."

I hope Burke caught that. I've already updated him on the report from Eve.

Teresa runs her hands up her tatted arms. "She was a good person. Just…hurting."

"How?" Burke asks.

"You know. Rough home life. Demanding parents. The sense that she never measured up."

Burke and I both nod, for our own reasons. He gets up and hands her his business card. "Thanks, Teresa."

"You're welcome. If you ever need breakfast, it's on the house." She winks at Burke.

Oh boy. But better him than me.

We walk out and Burke is standing on the steps, trying to visualize the attack, maybe, but my mind is two hours ahead, to the shakedown. "I need to go downtown and talk to a lead."

Burke is looking at me. "What about the Lexus?"

"I think we need to chat with Robert Swenson about how he knows Gretta." And since I already know the answer, I don't need to go, do I? He's her softball coach and owns a string of apartments in the area. Gretta stayed at a nearby apartment over the past three months. He's a legitimate businessman with a soft spot for the girls he coaches. And I know what you're thinking, but he has an alibi for the time of Gretta's murder—he was at home with his wife and fourteen-month-old son.

"Do you think Eve might have an address for Swenson from that stolen card?"

"Probably." For sure. I head toward my Camaro. "I'll meet you later."

"I have that gig tonight," Burke says. "The band is playing at the St. Paul Taproom."

Right. Burke is a drummer for a local jazz band, a hobby that's earned him the name, Sticks. Jazz doesn't do it for me, but I follow his gigs sometimes. Tonight, however, I'm out.

"Okay. I'll see you tomorrow, then."

"Are you sure you don't want to come with me?" Burke frowns. Maybe he's right, especially after my earlier diatribe, so—

"I do—but I have to follow up on a lead Booker gave me today." And that's sort of true, right? Booker did hand me the case files, did give me the watch...

I know I'm stretching it, but I don't like lying to Burke.

"Is it about your brother's case?"

It's about a cold case, so yes, in a way...

"Mmmhmm."

Don't judge me because you know you'd do the same thing.

Burke gets on his phone as he climbs into his car—probably calling Eve. I head back to the downtown precinct.

I park on the street, a little Aerosmith in my veins, telling me to Dream On, and I will, thank you. Across the street from Eve's building is the Adult Detention Center, and it's there that I ask about Jamal and Ari.

Jamal has been sprung, but Ari is a repeat offender and his bail is higher this time around. I wait for him in a small interrogation room with windows and he joins me, safely in chains, a young, rail thin twenty-something Somali man, wearing a wispy beard, his eyes reddened. I can recognize drug use when I see it. Ari is trembling, probably coming down hard from some high.

"Can we get him a glass of water, and—" I pull out a dollar bill. "A Snickers bar?" I ask this of the female security officer and she leaves us to retrieve it.

"Ari," I say. "How're you doing?"

"Do I know you?" He has an accent, his verbs pinched, tending toward the British slant.

"Nope. But I can help you. See, I'm looking for a guy named Hassan Abdilhali, and my guess is that you know him."

Ari looks away, his mouth tight.

"Did you know your buddy Jamal is already out?" I lean in. "Why is that, do you think?"

Ari lifts a shoulder.

The security officer returns with the water and candy and I put it in front of me. "Thanks."

She leaves again. We're being monitored, through the glass, and via a camera. That's fine. I don't have anything to hide. But I do have things to share. "Hassan Abdilhali is going to leave you here to rot while he builds his empire. Someday, he'll rule all the Somali gangs, and you'll be long forgotten, in jail for crimes he made you do."

Ari glances at me, then the water. His eyes linger a long time on the chocolate.

"It doesn't have to be that way. You tell me how to find Abdilhali, and I can make it easier on you in here." This is the part where I'm bluffing. I can't really do that, but I do have some pull with the county prosecutor. Don't ask me how, because it's a distant memory, but I'll do what it takes to get my information.

To get my life back.

I push the water toward him. "You help me, I help you."

Ari is staring at the water. Spittle has formed at the sides of his mouth, so I know he wants it. Bad.

He reaches for the cup but I move it back, out of his grip. "Ari?"

He looks at me. "He'll kill me."

"Not if he can't find you." I give him the water and he takes it, gulping it down.

Droplets glisten on his beard. A tiny spark has entered Ari's eyes.

I touch the candy bar. "I know you feel like no one cares about you. I know you're afraid. You come to this country hoping to find freedom, and instead you find more oppression—from inside your community, and out. But hatred only brings you more pain. Traps you in a cycle where you'll never break free." I push the candy toward him. "You gotta learn to trust people. To let them help you."

He's opening the candy bar.

"All I want to know is where I can find Abdilhali."

He's eating the candy bar now, but stops to look at me. "I want it in writing."

"I'll do better than that. I'll get you moved to a private cell. And tomorrow, I'll talk to the Wit-Sec program. You could start over. Would you like that?"

He takes a breath and inexplicably, his eyes fill. He looks away, and I do too.

This, I did not expect. But then again, when you find yourself too far down a path, rescue feels so improbable that when it shows up, it takes everything inside you to reach out for it.

Yes, I'm talking about me, too. Because I am starting to get glimpses of the man I was, or left behind in this timeline, and I'm keenly aware that I have this one chance.

No matter what happens, I'm holding onto Eve. I'm reaching out for help to Burke, and I'm going to fight the anger that has clearly overrun my life.

At least, I hope so.

"He operates out of a laundry in the Village West Market."

Of course he does.

"Thank you, Ari." I get up.

"I get my own cell, right?" He has drawn up one knee, wrapped his arm around it, and is holding on.

"I got ya," I say and gesture to the officer to let me out.

I stop by the warden's office, a man I haven't yet met, but I'm in the moment we shake hands. He's got a copy of The Last Year on his shelves, my New York Times best-seller, and I agree to an autograph for the small favor of putting Ari in a private cell, just for the night.

Tomorrow, I'll talk with Booker and see if we can get him better protection. Or better yet, I'll talk to Danny Mulligan.

Who is going to so owe me after tonight.

CHAPTER 12

Her father was going to murder her.

That might be going a little far. He was going to murder Rembrandt Stone. He'd just disown her.

What had she been thinking, inviting Rem to her family's Fourth of July party?

"Are you done with this sandwich?"

The voice jerked her back her microscope, where Eve was examining the cufflink she'd found on the street at Gretta's murder scene.

Silas picked up her bag, the other half of her ham sandwich inside. "Is this from that new deli down the street?"

"Yes," she said, then walked over and took the bag. "And no, I'm not finished."

"Looks good. What is it—ham?"

"Minced Ham Salad, my new favorite." Funny that Rembrandt knew that—it was such an odd filling for a sandwich. But he'd dropped it on her counter like he brought her lunch every day, the gesture familiar and easy.

Strange, but she felt exactly that way with Inspector Stone.

As if she'd known him all her life, the conversation between them fitting like an old shoe. Except, she barely knew the man, save for the hours and hours she'd invested in his memoir.

So maybe that was it—she knew him from his book. And perhaps their countless imagined conversations.

And one very delicious kiss.

Stop it.

She opened the bag now, and fished out the other half of the sandwich, aware of the beast inside her awakening with a frightening ferocity. What had Rembrandt said about being obsessed? You have to learn to take breaks, let your mind think. You get so focused on something it can keep you pinned to it, and then it will derail your entire life.

Yes, well, she'd spent most of her life focused and it had netted her a dream job with the Minneapolis Police Department, so maybe that wasn't a terrible crime.

More, her focused work had unearthed more than a few clues about Gretta's recent history. She unwrapped her sandwich and took a bite.

"Fine. I'll have to settle for a stale donut," said Silas. He had poured himself the last dregs of coffee and was now reading over the updated evidence board. "You tracked down the credit card in her possession."

"It wasn't hard." She came over to the board where she'd tacked a list of the charges. "It was registered to Robert Swenson, who owns property off of 41st Avenue South, just a few blocks away from Lulu's Diner. And, there's quite a few pizza delivery charges from Station Pizzeria, which is about four blocks to the east."

She'd printed out a map of the area and noted the locations with a marker. "My guess is she was renting out the place, or maybe just using it, but that's where she was living for the past three months."

"Who is Robert Swenson?"

"I ran his name, and of course we got about 726 hits in the Minneapolis area. But, when I ran his address, I found a Robert Swenson who coaches the Edina Hornets, a female fast-pitch community softball team."

"Do you think—"

"Yep. I did some digging and found an old picture of Gretta Holmes in uniform for St. Mary's Prep. She played shortstop."

"So, her coach found her a place to live."

"Looks like it." She took another bite of her sandwich. The afternoon sun hovered just over the horizon on its slow slide into the night, which put the time after dinner. Maybe she should head home.

Not be quite so, you know, obsessed.

Huh. She hadn't really noticed that about herself, but maybe Inspector Stone was onto something.

Funny, he almost knew her better than she did.

Funny, or creepy.

"Do you think they were...you know..." Silas raised an eyebrow.

It took her a second. Oh, Robert and Gretta. "Having a relationship? I don't know. He's married with a kid, so...let's hope he was just sincerely trying to help."

"Any updates on the cufflink?" Silas asked.

She finished her sandwich, wiped her hands on the napkin. "Yes. They're bronze cast, with nickel backings. Commemorative, with the crest of Sigma Chi, a Norman cross topped with an eagle holding a scroll in the middle. Their motto, In Hoc Signo Vincese is inscribed underneath."

"What does that mean?"

"In this sign, you will conquer."

"You looked that up?"

She frowned. "No. Didn't you study Latin?"

"Not even a little."

"How do you—never mind. The important part is the Sigma Chi at the top, and the year at the bottom—1855, the year they were founded."

They'd walked over to her microscope. "I was looking for any evidence, like skin or hair, but it's clean." She picked up a cloth and used it to retrieve the cufflink. "It looks hand cast, and I did some digging." She dropped the cufflink into a baggie. "Sigma Chi celebrated one hundred and sixty-five years of history last summer in a big nationwide to-do. All the living loyal life Sigmas who attended the event received a set of cufflinks."

"How many is that?"

"They've initiated over three hundred thousand members since inception, and about thirty-six thousand are categorized as lifers."

"How many in Minnesota?"

"I'm still trying to nail that down—I've requested a list of their current roster. There are three chapters in Minnesota, with over three thousand living loyal life Sigs according to their director. They had a local event as well as a national one. But I did track down an online picture of the group that attended here in Minneapolis." She lifted a color picture she'd printed. "I've asked for names of those who attended that, too."

"Is it an academic organization?"

She looked at him. "Silas. Did you ever walk frat row down at the U?"

"Only if I wanted to get ridiculed."

She knew him back then, skinny, glasses, the kind of guy who stayed indoors on weekends to study. "It's a big brick building next to Beta Theta Pi, and Phi Kappa Psi."

He gave her a blank look.

"Across from Folwell Hall."

"The foreign language department."

"And, Latin," she said, grinning.

"Right. I used to meet you there on Wednesday, right before we went to Stadium Subs in Dinkytown. And now I'm really hungry."

"Sorry, I finished my sandwich."

"I've been meaning to get down to the new deli. Did they have a big menu board?"

She made a face. "Inspector Stone brought the sandwich for me."

Silas gave her a look. "Really? So, after a month of cold shoulder, he suddenly warms up?"

"It's really the first time we've worked together since the bombing…" And, the thought just slid out. "You don't think he's just…"

"Trying to get on your good side?" He raised an eyebrow. "What do your instincts tell you, Brilliant Eve." He smirked.

So, he'd heard that. "I don't know."

"He's either Mr. Cold Shoulder, or Mr. I Need Your Help. C'mon Eve, he's just playing you."

"With a ham sandwich?" She gave him a face. "No. He was just being nice."

"Eve—"

"There's just something about him that makes me want to trust him."

"Trust? Or something else."

"Stop. He's smart. And a good detective. I know what you think of him—"

"What everybody thinks of him. Stone doesn't exactly have

a reputation for his sane thinking. I mean, who goes into a coffee shop that's about to be bombed?"

"A guy who is trying to save lives?" She didn't know why, but Silas's attack on Rembrandt bristled her. "Did you know they found the body of his brother just a month ago?"

"The one who disappeared when he was a kid?"

"He was twelve. They were out biking, and his brother was taken right off the road. They found him in a nearby lake."

"That's rough."

"So, maybe cut him a little slack. My guess is that grief like that might make a guy a little obsessed."

Silas considered her. Gave a slow nod. "Or a girl."

She met his gaze. She hadn't spoken often of her best friend, Julia Pike, murdered at fifteen. But, "Yes."

"Maybe you two are a good fit," Silas said, giving her a thin smile.

"There is nothing wrong with wanting justice, right?"

"Right." He finished his coffee.

"Besides, Burke certainly sticks up for him."

"Now there's a guy you should be into. Burke is solid. Honest. Dependable. The kind of guy you could bring home to your Dad without worry that he'll boot him out of the house."

"You sound like you have a crush on him," she winked.

"I'm just saying, as your friend, you could find a guy who wasn't so…"

"Focused?"

"Intense."

"I'm intense. Maybe Rembrandt and I are a good match."

"You're committed, in a forget-to-eat-dinner, go-without-sleep way. He's intense, as in, I'll-run-into-a-burning-building-and-I-don't-care-what-it-costs-or-whose-lives-fall-apart-because-of-it way. Big difference."

"He told me today that he's not like that anymore."

"Please. Rembrandt Stone has about as much ability to change as your father has the ability to stop hovering over you. Stone will always be a loose cannon, and one of these days, he's going to get someone killed. Like you."

She frowned at him, but the conversation wasn't so different from one she'd had with her father over a month ago when she started working for the 5th precinct.

When he'd warned her stay far, far away from Stone.

Instead, she'd flitted around the man like a moth to fire. Maybe her dad was right. All she knew was that if she showed up with him tomorrow night, fireworks would fly.

Talk about intense.

Probably she should call Rembrandt and tell him that…their house burned down. She'd moved to California. They'd all developed a case of measles.

Great.

"Let me know if we get a call back from Sigma Chi with those names," she said, and tucked the picture into her notebook.

Silas glanced at his watch. "You're leaving? It's only seven thirty."

"You're as bad as I am. Get a life."

She rolled the windows down on her Ford Escort as she headed home, the summer night filtering through her window. She toed off her shoes at a stoplight and drove the rest of the way barefoot.

Maybe Rembrandt would forget she asked. After all, it was Friday night. She'd simply not call him, and then, on Monday… oh, for the love…

It would help if the man didn't make her lose her common sense.

The buzz of a skill saw fractured the night as she turned down her street, a quaint south Minneapolis neighborhood at the juncture of Webster and Lake. She'd purchased the one-and-a-half story bungalow just a few months ago, in time for Samson, her brother, to decide to quit school and apply his budding remodeling skills to her bathroom, then her kitchen, and now, she hoped, to her backyard deck.

It was a cute house, with a bay window in front, the upstairs ceilings pitched, and a main floor office. Perfect for one person. Maybe a dog.

Although, Rembrandt Stone had fit rather nicely into her kitchen, hadn't he?

She pulled into the driveway, noticed the fresh cut grass, and followed the sound around to the back.

Sams wore a pair of cargo shorts, knee pads, his steel-toed work boots and a grimy t-shirt, his hat backwards on his head as he watched her kid brother, Asher, cutting a long piece of pine planking. Asher was dressed likewise, his hair pulled back in a ponytail, longer now, since school let out.

Fresh cement encased the footings, and an outline of boards formed the foundation.

Sams looked over at her. "Decided to get started on the deck."

"It looks amazing," she said, holding her hand up against the spray of sawdust.

Asher stood up, holding the board. "Hey, Sis."

"Cheap labor?" She asked Sams as Asher set the board in place.

"Couldn't let him sit around in front of his computer all day and get fat."

As if. Asher was lean and muscular from his hours waterskiing.

"I'm going to start painting the living room."

"Need any help setting up? Ash and I were just finishing up

128

for the night."

"No, I got this." She stepped through the deck toward the back door. Hoisted herself onto the step.

"Oh, Mom says not to forget the ice cream tomorrow night for the party. It's going to be a hot one."

Yes, yes it was.

She stepped inside, to the cool of her kitchen and set her satchel on the counter. Walked through to the dining room.

"Decided on a color yet?"

Sams had walked in behind her.

You might want to try Powell Bluff. I think you'll like it. For your dining room.

She sighed. Clearly there was no escaping Rem.

"Yes, I think I have. It's a sort of beige color."

Sams made a face of half-approval. "Could be good. It's hard to tell when it's in the can. You have to get it on the wall, let it dry, and see how it looks from every angle. You can't tell by the sample."

She looked at him. "Sams, that's just about the wisest thing I've ever heard you say."

He gave her a smile. "That's because I'm brilliant."

She laughed. "Yes, yes you are." Because maybe it was time for her father to meet the Rembrandt she knew instead of, well, the sample.

"See you tomorrow night, bro," she said. "And tell Mom, I won't forget to bring something delicious."

Everyone just had to calm down. Rembrandt Stone wasn't the off-the-hook guy they cast him to be. Everything was going to be just fine.

CHAPTER 13

In my timeline, the Phillips neighborhood still has a bad rap. Agreed, it has one of the highest murder rates in the city, and the gang activity has thrived here since the mid-sixties. But it's also the home of a private school, a block of gilded area historical mansions, the Minneapolis Heart Institute and St. Mary's University. More, it's the hub of immigration and a thousand delicious hole-in-the-wall restaurants with excellent take out.

My stomach is still whining as I pull up outside the Village Market. Thick in the air are the smells of turmeric, coriander and cumin, deep fried sambusas filled with ground beef, and I could easily eat a tray of Sabaayed slathered in honey.

Eve would be angry if I arrived home empty handed after a trip to Village Market. Although, in this time, the influx of Somalis is still young, many of them struggling to make ends meet (I suppose they still are in my time), and the gang activity is in its infant, dangerous and volatile stage.

And, in spite of our efforts, much of the violence is headquartered here.

The Village Market is a massive two-story warehouse that

covers an entire city block. Inside, the place is an under-roof market, with dozens of merchants hawking clothing, jewelry, pots and pans, household goods, bedding, shoes, cell phones, electronics and in every corner, food. Not just cafes, but coolers filled with goat meat and basmati rice, curry and fresh ginger, plantains and frozen grouper.

At the far end of the building is a Muslim prayer room, one for the men, and another, smaller one for women. And located at the other end, the laundromat where Hassan Abdilhali has set up shop.

In my time, Abdilhali owns half the market, (probably running some sort of protection service for the other half), as well as over two-dozen laundromats throughout south Minneapolis.

He's just a young thug now, however, and if Danny can take him down, he'll save countless lives. I hum to Fleetwood Mac, who is reminding me to go my own way—and turn into an alleyway off E 22nd street, a straight shot to the back door of the Market.

In the long shadows of an oak tree, Danny sits in his unmarked Ford Taurus, and I have to give him props for not driving a Crown Vic. Still, could he be more obvious? I don't know, but I get out, creep over to his vehicle, and tap on the passenger side.

He jerks his head toward me, a hint of fear on his face, but he recovers almost instantly. The look he shoots me could turn a man to dust, but I grin and motion for him to unlock.

His mouth pinches as I get in.

Because, you know, I'm going to save his stinkin' life tonight. He will like me, just you wait.

"What are you doing here?"

An empty coffee cup sits in the holder between the console seats. The cup is seated inside another cup, so maybe he's been here for a while. Might be a little overcaffeinated, if you ask me.

"Booker sent me." Lie, I know. "Said you might need back-up." Oh, the Chief will kill me if he ever finds out. But he won't. Hopefully.

I'm not sure, suddenly, if my actions might cause Booker to re-peal my chronothizing activities. What if he takes the watch away, in the future, as some kind of punishment? Or worse, never gives it to me in the first place? Would things revert to the beginning? Or would I be stuck in the world as I know it—?

Can't think about it, let it cloud my mind. I'm just going to stick to my plan.

"What?" Danny asks to my explanation. "How does Booker—"

"We've had our eye on Jamal and Ari," I say, and I'm such a smooth liar after years undercover, it can scare me. "When you tagged them last night, and then sprung Jamal, Booker got wind of it and sent me."

Danny stares at me a long moment, and I suddenly wonder if he can see right through me, all the way to my fifty-two-year-old, lying, bones.

"And he sent you?"

I raise a shoulder.

"Fine. Okay. Just. Don't. Talk to me." Danny settles back into his hundred-yard stare at the market building.

"So, what's the plan? Do you have Jamal wired? Sent him in to talk to Abdilhali? Aren't you worried Hassan is going to figure him out?"

Danny looks at me. "I guess now I am. What, are you psy-chic?"

Did I give away too much? I don't think so, I mean... "It's what I would do. Find an informant, get him close to the source, have the source give up some key information—like an upcoming drug shipment, right? And then..." I lift a shoulder.

Except, in the current version, something goes south and Danny ends up killing Abdilhali's brother.

Not tonight. I'll arrest the brother before Danny can end him. Let the courts handle the rest. "Ever had the sweet fry bread here?"

Danny glares at me, and frowns. "No."

"It's really good. Like a donut—"

"Stone?"

"Yeah?"

"Stop talking."

Danny has taken off his suit coat and tie, and rolled up his sleeves, like me. He has his window down, the smells of the evening wafting in, everything from the dust on the street to the lingering deep-fried smells from the nearby market. Now I notice that he's got an earpiece connected to a transceiver.

Whoops. But there's another earpiece wound up in the cup holder, so I take it and plug it in and in a moment, the voices are in my ear, too.

The conversation is in English, all tinged with that sharp Somali accent. Probably on purpose, although it's odd they're not speaking Somali, or even Arabic. I've heard that even in Somalia, Arabic is the primary language.

But English is the primary language of Minnesota, so…

There are four distinct voices in the room. I wonder which one is Jamal's until he says, "I just want to know where to meet, and then I will go."

Jamal. Worried, a hurry-up in his voice.

"What's your hurry, Jamal?"

The little hairs raise on the back of my neck because I recognize Hassan Abdilhali's voice. Deep, resonant and he's simply a younger version of the thug he will become.

He ran for city council last year and won. I remember watching the news wondering how many votes he paid for.

"No hurry. It's just—"

"I thought you were arrested last night." A different voice.

I cut a look at Danny.

"My sister posted bail. But I owe her. I need my money—"

"Where is Ari?" The voice has dropped, and this is again Hassan's.

"I don't know. Still inside, I think," Jamal says. "I...I'll go. I just...I just need my money, Hassan—"

"Where is my money, Jamal? The money you owe me for getting your family here, setting you up, taking care of you. I owe you nothing." And it's the lowering of his voice that has Danny—and me—taking a breath.

"He's in trouble," I say to Danny.

Danny cuts me a look. "He's okay. We just need the location—"

A gunshot, and Jamal's scream pierces through my brain. I yank out the earpiece—Danny does the same—and I'm out of the car. "You go around front!" I say to Danny, because if I were Hassan, I'd take the quickest exit out, and according to my mental blueprint, the laundromat is in the back.

I sprint for the back, past the ATM machines and into the building.

The place is still abuzz with activity, men and women shopping, a few merchants eying me as I slow to a walk and head straight for the Laundromax.

Hassan steps out into the aisle.

He doesn't know me, yet. And maybe never will. I was undercover for years in our previous life, trying to get close to the core of his operations. We took down a number of his cohorts, in a combined effort with the Chicago police department.

It's time for his rule to end, before it even gets started.

Now, in the shadows of the market, Hassan looks at me and I am angry enough to meet his eyes.

He takes off in a sprint. Because he's young—still in his late twenties—and doesn't have the clout to stand his ground.

I hate the idea of Jamal bleeding to death in the Laundromax—and that's when I spot Danny, huffing in behind me. "Get Jamal!"

We're off to the races. Thank you, O twenty-eight-year-old body.

If I can stop Hassan now, this whole thing ends. And maybe I change the world a little bit for the better for the Phillips neighborhood, too.

He cuts down an aisle with dresses hanging from the ceiling, but I'm just as young and fast—and frankly, as desperate—as he is. "Hassan, stop!"

A woman in his way goes flying, and another pulls her daughter from the path. They glare at me as I run by, as if this is my fault.

Hassan turns another corner—I mentioned that the market is like a maze, right?—and pulls down a display of pots and pans. They scream along the cement floor, skidding in my path, but I kick one, then another and plow through. "Hassan!"

I don't know why I'm yelling. It's not like screaming his name is going to slow him down.

We turn again, past a refrigerated unit of frozen meat, then again, past mountains of bedsheets in plastic that go careening into the aisle.

Then he sees daylight—a doorway at the end of the hall, propped open in the summer heat.

I can't shoot—not with a hundred spectators in every direction. So I dig down and find my forty-yard dash speed.

He hits the door just steps ahead of me, and I barely repress the urge to fly out and tackle him, but at the last second, I see he's jumped.

We're at a loading dock.

I fly off the end, arms windmilling, trying to keep from pitching forward.

Not a chance.

I land, trip, then duck and roll as I peel skin onto the gravel.

The wind leaves my body as I come to a stop.

I'm gulping like an Atlantic grouper, listening to Hassan's stupid feet pound the pavement. No—

Then my breath comes back with a whoosh and I gasp, roll over and force myself up.

The shot comes from behind me, a quick sharp report that echoes through me. It hits my bones and my knees buckle. I grip my chest, where it hurts the most.

Except, nothing.

I'm not hurt, no blood seeping between my hands. I gasp again, breathing hard, and turn around.

Danny is standing in the parking lot, at the edge by the alleyway. Crumpled between us is a man, face down, blood pooling beneath him where a bullet has ripped through him, center mass.

Not far away, just outside his grip is a handgun—what looks like a 9mm.

I stare at him, then at Danny, and I'm doing the math.

One of Hassan's men had the drop on me.

Danny Mulligan just saved my life.

I walk over to the man, lean down and check his pulse. Just because, well, maybe, right?

Not a chance.

Danny has walked over. He's staring past me, to where Hassan has vanished.

"Jamal?"

"Dead," Danny says. He is pulling out his radio.

I'm trying to get a good look at the man's face. He took a hard fall, and it's deformed and bloody. "And who is this?"

Danny toggles his radio, then pauses and stops. Looks at me, his mouth pinched. "That is Faheem Abdilhali. Hassan's first lieutenant and youngest brother."

Oh, man.

And as Danny walks away, I sink to the pavement and put my head in my hands.

CHAPTER 14

The paint color was perfect. A creamy yellow-beige that lightened up the entire room, contrasted with the dark wood baseboards and the freshly sanded original flooring.

It was like Rembrandt Stone had crawled inside Eve's head, taken a look around and knew her tastes exactly.

She puffed out a breath. No, not weird at all.

But it did make her feel like he knew her, understood her. That she wasn't making a gigantic mistake inviting him into her life.

Oh, she hoped.

She dropped the roller into the tray and took a step back, the odor of paint slipping out into the dark, fragrant night as she reached for her sweaty beer bottle.

From the radio on the floor, Celine Dion crooned out her Titanic hit, My Heart Will Go On. Eve had changed into cutoff shorts and a sleeveless shirt, and pulled her hair back. Now she ran her arm across her forehead, the heat of the evening gathering on her skin. She was hungry again, pizza on her mind—

A knock at the door nearly made her drop the bottle. Who

would be here now? She set the bottle on her dining room table and headed through the family room to the door.

Flicked on her porch light.

Really? Her stupid heart gave a rebellious little kick at the sight of Rembrandt standing on her porch, half turned away from the door, his hand cupped behind his neck, as if kneading a tight muscle.

She opened the door, and when he turned, she drew in a breath.

Blood stained his white shirt, open at the collar and he looked wrecked, a scrape on his forearm, one on his chin, and fatigue, or stress lines around his eyes.

"What happened!"

Rembrandt just sucked in a breath through his teeth.

"Are you okay?"

His jaw tightened, and he swallowed, then nodded.

Relief gusted out of her. Then, wait—"Is Burke okay?"

He nodded to that, too, frowning a little. "Yeah. He wasn't... he wasn't with me."

She held the door open and he glanced inside, back to her, as if not sure. "Come in, Rembrandt. You can't sit out here on the porch. The neighbors will start talking."

He stepped inside. Glanced at the dining room.

"Painting."

"Good color choice."

"I knew you'd like it."

No comment there. She gestured to the sofa. "Want a beer?"

His gaze went to her bottle, sitting on the table, then he shook his head. "Water."

Huh. She went to the kitchen.

He followed her, and the sense of him in her space, this man who embodied both mystery and the eerie aura of home sneaked under her skin and stayed there.

She didn't hate it, or the way his presence made every cell in her body buzz.

He was a handsome man, even in his untucked state.

Oh, for Pete's sake, calm down.

She filled the glass with ice, then water and handed it to him. He drank it down and set it on the counter.

"Want to talk about it?"

He shook his head.

Right. "Want something to eat?"

"If I eat, I'll just...no." His gaze had gone to a picture on her counter and he seemed fixed on it.

"That was taken a month ago, during my Dad's annual birthday party."

"Yeah," he said, like he knew about it. Maybe he did because the event was sort of legendary in the force. A big blowout every year on the lake.

He'd been in the hospital during the party this year.

Rembrandt turned away from the picture and looked out to the backyard. "Samson has started on your deck."

Last time he'd been here, Sams was working on the kitchen tile. "He pulled in Asher to help."

"How is he?"

"Sams?"

"Asher. Did he get into any trouble sneaking back into the house?"

Ah, Rembrandt was referring to last month's sneak and grab of Asher to do some hacking into a database of coffee distributors. "No," she said and walked back into the dining room to grab her beer. "He seems to know the ropes. Has a ladder right outside his window, if that isn't obvious. But my dad seems to have rules only for his daughter. Even if she is twenty-six and can fend for herself."

Right then, Mariah Carey came on the radio, singing Always Be My Baby, and Rembrandt looked at her, his expression almost stripped, and raw.

"Are you all right?" She walked over to turn off the radio—

"Leave it," Rem said quietly, his voice a low rumble. He leaned against her door frame, his hands in his pockets. He wore a five o'clock grizzle on his chin, his hair roughed up. And despite his youth, his gaze held something deeper, an appreciation, maybe, in his deep blue eyes. It sent a dark simmer under her skin. "You have paint on your chin."

She touched her face.

"I got it." He came over and used his thumb to wipe it away. Then he cleaned it on his already stained shirt.

"Rem—whose blood is that?"

"It's the brother of a drug lord named Hassan Abdilhali."

"What happened?" She touched his arm—oh, he had a nice bicep there.

He took a breath and moved away from her, something terrible in his eyes.

"You're scaring me."

"Sorry." He made a face, that hand behind his neck again. "I probably shouldn't have come here. I just…I'll go."

He headed toward the front door.

She caught him at the door, shutting it on him. "I'm glad you came by. Sit down and tell me what happened."

She took his hand and urged him toward her stairs. Sat on them. Patted the space next to her.

After a moment, he sank down to join her. Then he pressed his hands to his face and didn't speak for a long moment.

She hadn't known him long, but she understood the non-verbal language of a man trying to process tragedy. Or worse, the bone-shaking terror of a near-miss.

Something bad, very bad, had gone down.

Her heartbeat filled the silence.

Finally, "I thought I'd fixed it, Eve. I really thought…" Rembrandt sighed, looked at her, and she jolted at the wetness in his eyes. "I just…I don't want to…" He swallowed again. "You have to believe that I really thought I could fix this. That I could keep your Dad safe—"

"My dad?" She stilled. "What about my dad?"

"He's fine." Rembrandt held up his hands. "He's just fine. In fact…" He winced, then met her eyes again. "He saved my life."

Oh Rem. She longed to touch him, and then couldn't stop herself from pressing her hand to his chest. "Tell me," she said softly.

He didn't want to—she could tell by the way he closed his eyes, looked away, then back at her, so much torture in his gaze.

But she didn't remove her hand, and held herself back from letting him off the hook. Added, "Please."

His voice turned low. "We were on a stakeout. Your dad wired up an informant, and sent him in, looking for information on a gang leader—Abdilhali. Suddenly, everything went south. We heard a gunshot and I took after Abdilhali. Chased him through a warehouse, came out the other side and that's when your dad showed up. He blew a hole through his brother, Faheem Abdilhali."

"Faheem had the drop on you?"

"Yes. Your dad shot him center mass, a second before he would have taken me out."

"Are you okay?"

He swallowed. Nodded. "I'm just—"

"Freaked out."

He blinked. "I—"

She didn't know why, but she had the sense that the unflappable Rembrandt Stone was unraveling before her eyes.

She framed his face with her hands. Met those blue eyes. So many layers, but she focused on the place inside that was the cop, the guy who put himself out there for people, for justice. The guy who didn't think about himself until it was too late. "You're okay, Rem. You're safe. Just breathe."

He stared at her.

And then, he kissed her. A full on, no hesitation kiss, as if he was starving and she was the nourishment he needed. He clasped his hands on either side of her head, drinking her in, and shoot, the man was dangerously intoxicating, the taste of him, reckless and yes, intense.

Oh, she liked intense way too much.

She fisted her hand into his shirt and pulled him closer, his heart pounding against her touch. He smelled of the night, the slightest layer of sweat, and not a little coffee and yes, he maybe even scared her a little, but she didn't hate it.

Not at all. Something about this man ignited places inside her that she never knew existed. And this—this—was what no one knew about Rembrandt Stone. The man wore his heart on the outside of his body, intense, yes, but had the kind of passion that told her that when he was in, he was all in.

Then, just like that, he pulled away, staring into her gaze, breathing hard. "Sorry. I just…I just…"

"Shh. Calm down, Rembrandt. I don't hear anyone shouting stop."

He raised an eyebrow then, his eyes widening. "Right." He scooted away. "Maybe you should. You barely know me, Eve."

Funny, the way he said, it sounded like he knew her, however.

"I know you're a good man. A man who is committed to justice and that when I'm with you, I feel safe."

His jaw tightened and he looked away again. Ran his thumb under his eyes.

"It's going to be okay." She touched his shoulder.

"No, it's not." He turned back to her.

Oh. Right. "I'll bet my dad is foaming at the mouth."

"It's not pretty. He thinks I screwed up his operation. That Hassan is going to pack up and move, and it'll take months to find him again and set up another possible sting. But that's not the worst—"

"You need to back out of the party tomorrow night." She got it, really. "You're probably right."

His mouth opened. "No, I mean—yes, you're dad is there, but—I need to be there."

"Rem, I think maybe we need to rethink that. I mean, I want you to join us, but after tonight—"

"I'm going to your party, Eve."

Really.

He held up a hand. "Sorry. I didn't mean to…" He sighed. "I think your dad is in danger."

She frowned.

"Hassan will retaliate. And, I think he'll try to murder your father."

She froze. "Does he know my father is the one who killed his brother?"

Rembrandt stilled, as if considering her words. Then, "Uh, I don't know. Maybe not. Maybe Hassan didn't see it. And no one else was around…"

"Then he doesn't know who pulled the trigger."

He looked at her and one side of his mouth tweaked up. "No, he doesn't. You're right." He blew out a breath. "Huh."

He started for the door.

"Rem!"

He stopped, his hand on the knob, and turned at her voice.

"You don't have to protect me," she said.

The look he gave her undid her, reached right in and took a hold of her heart, pulling it from her body. "Yes, I do, Eve. Because if I lose you, I lose everything."

The way he said it was as if he'd felt that way for ages.

And then he left.

She sank down on the step, her heart thundering.

The man simply didn't play fair.

CHAPTER 15

You can't win against time. Booker is in my head as I stare at my ceiling of my one-bedroom, third floor apartment. The orange glow of the sunrise is barely glinting my windowsill and the wind teases the blinds, smacking them against the screen.

I can smell rain.

I was here three days ago, in my time, and then the place was fairly immaculate, given my bachelorhood status.

When I arrived last night, the tiny vintage apartment looked like it had been hit by my college self, with a couple empty pizza boxes on the table and more than a few socks balled up and thrown at the television set, a stained white t-shirt hanging on a radiator.

I spent a few minutes tidying up for the young man inside me who seems to be having a hard time getting back on his feet. Take out the trash, wash the dishes, throw the clothes into the wash.

If I'm going to rewrite my life, I should do it in clean duds.

Mostly I had to work out of my system the desperate urge to return to Eve's house, to find myself again on the stairs, kissing the woman who still believes in me.

I admit to losing a piece of myself, holding onto Eve as if she belonged to me—and enjoying way too much the fact she seemed to want me, too. She is young and compassionate and I'm a jerk because someday she's going to sit on a picnic table and tell me it hurts her too much to love me.

Yeah, that thought was in my head, too, as she kissed me. And maybe I dove in because I wanted to expunge that impulse from her thoughts.

Then she said the thing that turned me cold. "He doesn't know who pulled the trigger."

No. Hassan might not know it was Danny who shot his brother.

He might even think it was me.

It was that thought that drove me out of her house to my tiny apartment. It settled in a dark and jagged place in my brain. Itched at my attempts at sleep.

What if I screw up, do something stupid here and die? Do I just vanish? Clearly if Art is right, and I'm overwriting time, then yes. Finito. I'm just a memory in Eve's rear-view mirror.

Ashley never exists.

But that's not why I can't sleep. Well, not the only reason.

I keep running the fight with Booker through my head. The real fight we had in my very real past three years ago before I quit the force.

The night I watched Jimmy Williams get gunned down by a fifteen-year-old gang member in an ambush...twenty years from now.

He was one year from retirement, left behind two teenage children, and seeing his wife at his funeral made me return to the station and turn in my badge.

Yes, just like that. Ashely was four and I was shaken to the bone.

Booker tried to talk me out of it in a heated, you're-a-cop-for-life argument. How being a cop is more than a job. It's a responsibility, a calling.

That it was in my soul.

Maybe. But I had a family, a life.

Had being the key word for me, pounding in my brain as I tossed the night away.

I had a life.

And I came here knowing I would do anything to get them back.

But again, not if I'm dead.

The sound of the gunshot in the parking lot is also ricocheting in my head, along with the odor of blood on my hands, and the cold slick of horror that if Danny had listened to me, I would be dead.

I break out in a cold sweat every time that thought passes over me.

So, there's a crowd of voices in my brain, and needless to say I don't sleep well.

When dawn breaks through the high transom windows in my bedroom, I get up and take this body out for a run around the lake.

Might as well enjoy it while I can.

The run airs out my brain too, and I'm not quite so edgy as I climb up the three flights and enter my newly cleaned apartment.

Listen, I mutter to myself. No one died yesterday.

And no one is going to die today.

And as long as I save Danny and Asher, and manage not to get myself killed, everything will be just fine.

My machine is blinking and I retrieve my messages as I strip off my shirt and stick my head in my fridge, searching for sustenance.

Two cans of beer and a piece of moldy cheese sit forlornly in my fridge. I hadn't realized that I had such serious issues with eating healthy.

"Rembrandt, this is Mom."

Oh, boy. I throw out the beers and the cheese and close the fridge. I haven't talked to Mom—well, maybe I have, but you know what I mean—since the police found my brother's body a month ago. I left this time almost immediately after solving the cold case last time—and that realization hits me. Timing.

What if I save Danny and Asher's life and never find Gretta's killer?

"Aunt Joann and Uncle Bert have stopped by, and we're all having brunch this morning," my mother says from the machine.

My mother's sister and her husband. Nice, God-fearing folks from Brainerd. I have a couple fond memories of ice-fishing with Uncle Bert. I check the freezer and find a burrito. It's icy around the edges, having had a long quiet life behind the ice trays.

"We're hoping you can stop by and join us. I haven't seen you in weeks, not since the hospital…" She pauses, and I still.

They must have come to the hospital to visit me after the stabbing. Or maybe…what if, despite all I did, she still had her stroke? I can't remember now, my memory foggy and I close the freezer door in a rush of fear.

"I hope you're feeling better. I…we miss you."

The message ends and I stare at the machine.

They miss me? This is new. After Mikey vanished, life simply halted while my parents searched, grieved, searched, grieved more… an endless cycle that I eventually stepped out of and watched.

They never really noticed my absence.

Not that I blamed them. No one actually pointed any fingers at me, at the fact that we were out biking together, me, the older brother, and Mikey, three years younger, struggling to catch up to me.

Then he was gone, and you know the rest.

Probably I need to check in with my family and see what damage I've done to them. See what I can do to fix it.

You can't win against time.

Yeah, yeah I heard you.

I shower and dress, pulling on a pair of clean jeans—thank you fresh laundry—my favorite band t-shirt, a relic I picked up while attending a Journey concert, slip on my Cons and I'm out the door.

I've forgotten, really, the ebullient sense of youth, how it fills your pores and makes you believe you're invincible. Maybe the young me is in here somewhere, because my panic from Eve's words last night has dissolved.

Journey reminds me to keep the faith as I crank Don't Stop Believin' and I take Highway 7 out to Waconia, a small town about thirty minutes from the city. My parents live on a small hobby farm, with a barn my father uses for his vintage car repair. My 1988 Porsche sits under a tarp, waiting for a rebuilt carburetor and a number of other problems, and I suddenly miss it.

Truth is, I kept the car at the farm as an excuse to see my parents. I would come out to work on the car mostly when Eve and I were in our off-again moments and it became a time when my father and I talked about everything that didn't matter, but of course it seriously mattered.

Because at least we were talking.

Now, as I pull up to the yellow, two story house with black shutters, the grass is mowed, the front garden has been weeded, the rose bushes cut back and red geraniums spill out of planters on the wide porch.

The place looks downright cheery.

I pull in next to a dirty caravan with a Brainerd International Raceway sticker on the back window.

By the time I climb out, my mother has emerged onto the porch.

The sight of her causes me to brace my hand against the roof of the Camaro. Mom?

She's wearing a pair of jeans, a sleeveless shirt and flip flops. She's lost weight. Put on makeup. Her dark red hair is down around her face and she's sporting a tan.

My mother hasn't worn makeup since she attended my high school graduation.

More importantly, she's smiling. "Rembrandt!" She holds open her arms and I resist the urge to look around, maybe to spot another version of myself who she's excited to see.

She comes off the porch and her arms circle my neck before I know what to do. "You got my message!"

She feels strong and bright and radiating an energy that stirs up Booker's words. This...gift...is to help give people closure. To let them live in peace.

Peace. Maybe that's what it is. A release of the lethal, dark grip of living in limbo.

I hug her back and she gives me a kiss and yes, maybe Booker is right. This might be enough.

Might.

"Your uncle and aunt are inside, but your father is in the barn. I think he's working on your car." She pats my cheek. "Go say hi."

I'm now, apparently, a member of the Cleaver family. "Sure," I say and head out to the barn.

Once upon a time, my father and I, along with Mikey, would spend Saturdays covered in grease, rebuilding engines, taking apart carburetors, and changing the oil in whatever beaters my father was currently rebuilding. He had a fling with a few VW bugs, then upgraded to Audis.

No wonder I fell in love with Porsches.

All of my memories include sweaty cans of grape Fanta, my father's cloth-covered Panasonic radio screaming out Seger, and Mikey trying to sword fight me with one of my father's Pittsburgh 1/2 inch torque wrenches.

I step into the shadows of the barn with some trepidation.

He's got the tarp off the Porsche, the trunk is up and he's leaning inside, looking at the motor. "What happened to this thing anyway?"

"The engine died after a high-speed chase."

"It's running rough. Sounds like it's hitting only a couple cylinders."

The familiar smell of engine oil mixes with the scents of dirt and age in the barn, and I almost hear the echo of Mikey's voice. Ghosts. I stick my hands in my pockets, fighting a shiver.

"Yep. The timing belt is loose." Dad leans up. "My guess is that it jumped a tooth on the right bank. We'll have to loosen it up and take a look."

Dad is wearing a pair of old work pants, an oily flannel shirt and his cap on backwards over his thinning hair. He goes to his work bench and lifts a cup of coffee from the ancient green thermos. "It's a pretty car, though. I can see why you like her."

It's like we're continuing a conversation I can't remember. "Thanks."

He returns to the car. "Hand me a 10mm ratchet."

I walk over to his standing toolbox and pull out the drawer with the ratchets. My father is an electrician, but he knows cars and keeps his tools immaculate.

I find the ratchet and hand it to him. The transistor is belting out a little Steely Dan—Do It Again—and suddenly I'm twelve.

"You look like you took one on the chin, Rem." He takes the bolts off the timing belt cover and removes it.

"Had a little scuffle chasing a suspect last night."

"Give me the 22 mil."

I find it and he uses it to turn the crank shaft to align the timing marks on the pulley with the engine pointer.

"Are the left cam shaft timing marks aligned?"

I stick my head into the engine. I know he can see these for himself, but maybe he also thinks I'm still twelve. "Yep."

"So, did you get him?"

"Nope." I don't want to tell him the rest. "He's still at large. The right timing marks are off."

"It's what I thought—timing belt's jumped. We'll have to re-align it."

It occurs to me in a not-funny way that that's why I'm here—to realign time. Or, rather, to make it run better.

"Funny that just one tooth off can make a car run so rough and send it out of commission."

I stare at him. That's it, of course. One tooth is off in my spectacular plan to fix time. Maybe I already fixed it, though. If Hassan doesn't know Danny is the shooter, then maybe he never sends the drive by.

As for me, well…I'll just have to watch my back. Funny, the chill of death seems to have dissipated with the sunlight.

Dad glances at me. "You okay?"

"Yep."

"You working on any big cases?" He's loosening the timing belt tensioner to allow slack.

"A murder case. A young woman—runaway, we think. Her

parents have been searching for her for three months." The words are out before I can snake them back, and I'm suddenly keenly aware of my father's own fruitless search for Mikey. But he just nods as he slides the belt off the right cam shaft sprocket.

"The poor parents. It's terrible to wonder every night where your child is. You spend all your time trying to figure out if you could have done something different, rewriting your responses, imagining a different outcome." He loosens the timing belt tensioner to get slack, then turns the cam shaft back a tooth. "At least now they know." He puts the belt back on and I watch in silence, my heart a fist in my chest.

I take a breath, not sure if I want to ask the question.

Frankly, not sure if I want the answer either. "Would you do things differently, Dad? Now that you know."

He pauses for a sec, then stands as he gingerly pulls his wrench out, relaxing the tension on the old motor.

"I don't know, son. As a father, you can't ever give up. It's in your bones. You can't stop caring. The only way you survive is to hang onto hope. Otherwise, your life becomes despair."

He bends back over the engine. "But I also believe that everything happens for a reason, and to ignore that reason and start over is to miss the lesson."

I shake my head. "What lesson can be learned by Mikey's death, Dad. C'mon."

He glances over and meets my eyes. "Even in tragedy there are lessons, Rem. Everyone has something in their past they'd like to redo. It doesn't mean it should be redone. Our mistakes, our tragedies, our suffering make us better, stronger, more compassionate people. And those are lessons we learn by going through the pain, not around it."

He leans up again, grabs a rag to wipe the wrench. Looks

away. "But if I had to do it over, I might not have obsessed so long on finding the son I lost, to the detriment of the one I still had."

A hand has pressed my chest and I can't breathe. I nod, and also look away—

"I'm going to crank the engine over a couple times, then align the marks again. Take a look and see if all three line up."

Somehow, I do, although my eyes are blurry. "Yep. All aligned."

"Let's fire it up. You left the keys in the ignition."

I get inside and crank the engine over. It catches, but sputters and hiccups, as if trying to die.

Dad comes around. "I think we have a bigger problem here." He wipes his hands. "We'll have to pull the spark plugs and do a compression test. But I'm fresh out of coffee and I'll bet your mother's cinnamon rolls are ready."

I have a vague memory of those, and it's enough for me to climb out of the car.

"We can tackle it after breakfast." He turns to put his tools away. And for the first time I notice that he still has hair, blonde and thin, yes, but sticking out the back of his hat. Blue eyes, but they hold a peace that I don't recognize.

"It's a good thing you didn't get one of those new fancy Lexus models. Toyota." He shakes his head. "At least a Porsche has good bones."

His automotive prejudices coming through. But I grin and nod.

His words from before, however, ping back to me. It's terrible to wonder every night where your child is. As a father, you can't ever give up. It's in your bones. You can't stop caring.

In my head, I'm getting out of the Camaro at HCMC, noticing a Lexus in the lot.

The one that belongs to Jeff and Karen Holmes.

forc

give a quick

coming by,
take out the
s up. It's just
car is giving

e.
gy. That's right,
I think I know

CHAPTER 16

I've not only figured out the case by the time Burke arrives at the Edina home of Jeff and Karen Holmes, but I've worked up a serious head of steam, too.

The Holmes' place is nice. An older white colonial, with black shutters and a circle drive. The tall cedar trees flanking the yard suggest money.

In my time, we'd be looking at a 1.5 mil retro fixer upper. Now, it's a cool million, and I'm wondering what went on inside to cause Gretta to run.

I have some ideas, and they're dark, so I don't want to entertain them. But a guy in my line of work can't rule anything out.

So, I'm sitting in my car, my arms folded, just barely resisting the urge to stalk up the driveway and take Jeff Holmes apart.

Asia's, Heat of the Moment isn't helping. And yes, it's the young, impetuous me inside roaring to life, but it's the old me, too, the me who has lost a daughter.

The me who can't imagine a father who would hurt his own child.

Burke has pulled up behind me. He gets out and walks over to me just as I get out, too. "What's up?"

I can't stop myself. "The father did it."

Burke glances at the house, then back at me. "You get roughed up last night?" He's staring at my chin.

"Took a spill. Listen, here's how—"

"Were you on a case?"

What? "No—yes, sorta, but—listen to me—"

"Without me?"

I give him a look. "I was helping Danny Mulligan with a stakeout. You had a gig. Whatever."

Burke frowns, and his jaw tightens. "Yeah, whatever. What are we doing here?"

Thank you. "The Lexus."

"And?"

"In Lulu's parking lot. Teresa remembers seeing it, early, before Gretta's shift."

"Yeah?"

"I think it belongs to Gretta's father."

Burke draws in a breath. "He didn't mention seeing her—"

"C'mon. The mom knew where she was. She'd been giving Gretta money for weeks through her softball coach."

"When did you—I haven't even written my report of the interview yet."

Shoot. That's right. We didn't find that out until after we'd questioned Robert. Or rather, Robert's wife, Angie. She let that little piece of information slip out after he left the house to attend softball practice for this weekend's tournament.

So, what am I going to do? "Karen told us. Remember? Yesterday?"

Burke narrows his eyes as I hustle on. "My thinking is that Dad found out where she was and tracked down her location from

Mom, then went to find her. Maybe he wanted to ask her to come home." And then it occurs to me. "What if he knew she was pregnant? And they got in an argument—"

"And she got out of the car, and started to run? But where did the strangling come in?"

"I don't know. Eve said the bruises were old." And now, our conversation rings back to me. What if the guy in the car was the father of her child? Maybe she told him she didn't want an abortion, and they got in a fight.

No. Please no. Because if Jeff Holmes is the father of his daughter's child—I can't even think it.

I turn and stalk up to the house. Burke runs after me. "Rem—what's going on?"

"Nothing. I just want to ask him where he was the morning of his daughter's murder."

"You don't look like you're in a just asking mood." He puts his hand on my shoulder, but I shrug him off.

"Rem—"

I round on him, hold up my hands. "Chill. I have full containment."

But when we ring the door and it opens, I'm not so sure. Jeff Holmes is wearing golfing clothes—a yellow shirt with a green Burl Oaks Golf Club logo on the breast, a pair of white pants, and is clearly headed out for a nice day on the course.

While his wife grieves their dead daughter?

I nearly push him into the house while Burke explains that we have more questions.

I just have the one. "Where were you yesterday morning around 6 o'clock?"

He frowns at me, probably trying to stir up an alibi. I hope he sees the warning in my eyes.

"Jeff? What's going on?"

Jeff turns to his wife, who has come down the stairs. She's wearing a yellow summer sweater, a golf skirt, her hair back in a headband and I can barely take it in.

Who are these people?

"Detective Stone seems to think I had something to do with Gretta's death." Jeff snaps and looks at me.

Burke's hand again lands on my shoulder.

He talks because my words are balled in my chest. "We just need to clear up a few more questions," he says. "Paperwork."

Karen joins her husband. "We answered all your questions." But wariness hovers in her eyes, as if afraid we'll pry too deep.

She's probably protecting Jeff, and that burns me.

We're standing in a living room, just off the entry, with a grand piano, a glass coffee table, flanking white linen sofas, and a wall of pictures. I walk over to the wall.

"You haven't answered the one I just asked." I glance over my shoulder at Jeff. Raise an eyebrow.

"I was running," he says. "Every Friday morning, I take a longer run while Karen has a breakfast with her friends."

"Anybody see you?" Burke asks.

"I suppose." He shrugs. "I don't know."

I do. I turn back to the pictures on the wall. They're the usual pictures of Gretta at all ages—cute girl, who went through her buck-toothed stage—and some of the entire family. They had a springer spaniel at one time. "Gretta is an only child?"

Karen walks over. "Yes. She was adopted. We couldn't have children of our own."

"She looks like a good girl," I say. "Did she get into trouble?"

Karen is quiet. "Until recently, she seemed very happy. Then, she started acting out. Getting moody. I think she was depressed.

She ran away three months ago, after a terrible fight."

"But you knew where she was." I'm still looking at the pictures. There's one with grandparents, a picture taken on the lake. And another with her standing by a grand piano, in a gold-gilded room. "This one. Where was it taken?"

"At orchestra hall. She was a gifted pianist, and she and a few other students had a private concert. She only invited one other couple to the event."

"Who?"

"Her softball coach and his wife." Karen touches the picture, and her voice turns low. "They've been very good to us."

"They gave her a place to stay, didn't they? At one of their rental units."

She meets my eyes. Nods, something of fear in her expression. My gaze flicks to Jeff. He's watching us, his mouth tight.

"That's how you knew where she was," I say quietly to him.

He swallows. "No," he says. "I didn't know where she was."

He's lying. I turn back to the wall.

"Then why was your Lexus at Lulu's yesterday morning?" Burke asks.

There are more pictures, of Jeff and Karen in their youth, little Gretta on Karen's lap. And their wedding picture, Karen looking young and pretty in a flouncy dress.

My gaze lands on another picture.

Jeff Holmes, undergrad, sitting on the steps of his fraternity at the University of Minnesota.

Sigma Chi.

My gut tightens because I knew it. I was an idiot to not see it the first time, but we didn't have the cufflink, or the Lexus sighting, and somewhere in the back of my mind, maybe we didn't even dig into the alibi—I don't want to know where we screwed up.

I just know we did.

I turn, my eyes hard on Jeff. "You went to Sigma Chi."

He nods, his gaze hitting the picture.

I take a step toward him. "Did you know Gretta was pregnant?"

His mouth opens, and he looks at Karen, then back to me. "What?"

Of course, I don't know she was pregnant, not for sure, but just in case— "She visited an abortion clinic the morning of her death. And you knew it. Because you were waiting for her in the Lulu's parking lot. Probably saw her coming down the street from the clinic. And maybe she saw you and because your wife had been giving her money, she was probably relieved to see you, hoping you'd shown up to help her, to rescue her...except, were you?"

Jeff is just standing there, his mouth closed, his Adam's apple dropping in his throat.

I know guilt when I see it. "You went to see her, didn't you? What, to tell her to come home? Or maybe...maybe you gave her money to have that abortion." I haven't mentioned the twenty dollar bill in her grip.

His breath hiccups, and I don't care. I take a step toward him. "Why did she run away from home, Jeff? You said it was because you two fought over her boyfriend. But was it really because she didn't feel safe? Maybe...because you were the father of her child?"

I should have expected the right hook, given the dark look in the man's eyes. The punch is flimsy at best.

It barely stings, and I step back, ready to round on him.

But he roars and leaps on me, and suddenly, I'm back peddling and slamming into the glass coffee table.

The thing shatters, and Jeff is on top of me.

I let him have another lick because I can't figure out a way to get him off me without tearing myself to shreds.

And I'm remembering Jeff's strange behavior at the morgue. Despair? Or something else?

Maybe a desire not to live in limbo anymore.

Enough to park his Lexus outside Lulu's? Maybe force his daughter to come home?

"Dad. I gotta go." I take him by the shoulders and give a quick squeeze. "I'm so sorry. Tell mom I'll give her a call later."

He stares at me, still holding the rag. "Thanks for coming by, son. We'll get your car running, even if we have to take out the head, replace the valves, and rebuild it from the bones up. It's just a matter of staying the course, reading the clues the car is giving you."

What he said.

I stalk toward my car, pulling out my cell phone.

Burke picks up on the fifth ring, his voice groggy. That's right, he had a gig last night.

"We need another go-round with Jeff Holmes. I think I know why he looked like he wanted to murder someone."

I just hope it wasn't his own daughter.

Then Burke is on him, pulling him up.

I find my feet and he breaks away from Burke and comes at me again. This time, I bat his hand away, the wimpy golfer that he is, grab his other arm, twist him around and in a second, he's against a wall, his arms behind him, in cuffs.

"No!"

Karen might have been screaming this entire time, but I haven't heard her until now. She is crying and shouting as she rushes Jeff.

Burke catches her. "Calm down. He's not under arrest—"

"Yes he is," I say. "He attacked me—"

"It wasn't him!" Karen is trying to unlock Burke's arms from around her waist. "It wasn't him at Lulu's—it was me!"

Everyone stills as we look at her.

"I didn't kill my daughter! But I did go there to plead with her to talk to me. To come home and let us...let us help her." She's crying now and gone is the woman of poise. Her headband is torn free, her eyes blackened, mascara running down her face. "She called me to meet her, but she never showed up. And I didn't want Jeff to know—"

"I knew." His voice is quiet and for the first time, I see a man broken, a man beyond the golf shirt, the perfect hair, the million-dollar home. "I knew you were visiting her."

"How?" Karen's eyes fill.

"I heard you talking to her. And I knew you were giving her money. But I just..." He closes his eyes. "I just thought, in time, she'd come home."

Oh. Denial. I'm painfully familiar with that game. For a moment, I'm standing in the middle of my kitchen, looking at an empty bottle of Macallans.

"Are you sure she was pregnant?" His eyes are fierce even as they cloud over.

I have a terrible, sinking feeling.

"Not for sure," Karen whispers. "Why?"

He shakes his head. "I don't trust him."

And I know who, even as Burke asks.

"Robert Swenson," I say, and Jeff nods.

"I think he talked her into leaving. I think maybe…maybe he was sleeping with her. We had it out a few weeks ago, before a game. He was coming from some deal he made, all cocky, like he was some hotshot, and I confronted him." Jeff takes a breath. "He told me that my daughter didn't belong to me anymore. That she was eighteen and could make her own choices."

"And what did you say?"

"We scuffled, but I…" He looks at me, then Karen. "I loved Gretta. I would never hurt her. And I feared that he might say something to her to make her push us out of her life."

"A father never stops caring." I don't know why I'm channeling my father. "The only way you survive is to hang onto hope."

Jeff looks at me like I get it. And I do. Oh, wow, I do. More, I'm doing some scant math. What if during the scuffle, his cufflink fell off, lodged into the door of the Lexus? And maybe, while Karen was at Lulu's it fell out…

Before I can test this theory, however, I hear a voice.

Oh no.

"Did you call Booker?" I hiss to Burke, who frowns at me, but Booker strides in before I get an answer.

"Stone!" His voice rings out again. I slowly look up at him.

"Yeah."

"We got a 9-1-1 call from a neighbor," Booker says, "And dispatch ran a search on your cars. Placed you both here." He walks over to Jeff, looks at me. "Wanna tell me what's going on?"

He's giving me a hard look, and for some reason, I feel like his arrival has something to do with our previous conversation, the one about changing time. I shake my head. "Following up on a case."

"And?" He looks at Jeff.

I'm unlocking the man's cuffs. Mostly because I believe him, and yes, he took a swing, or two, at me, but you were there. You heard what I said. So, "You good?" I ask Jeff.

He rubs his wrists, glances at Booker, then nods. "We have an alarm system. You can check the time I returned from my run. My wife was back from her breakfast—or I guess, her visit to Lulu's—by then."

My hunch is that it's long before we showed up at Lulu's to find Gretta's body still warm.

Which means, I'm still looking for a killer.

Booker glances at me, and gestures with his head. And I know I'm in for it when we step out on the stoop and he shuts the door behind me.

He purses his lips, puts his hands in his pockets. He's wearing his badge on a lanyard around his neck, his leather jacket, and that watch on his wrist. My watch.

I want to ask if he's done any traveling lately.

"I know where you were last night."

My head pops up and all I can think was…Eve?

"You went to that stakeout with Danny to stop him from getting killed."

Yeah, I did. But here's the thing. If he believes that I stopped Danny's murder, then maybe he won't get his knickers in a knot when I go over to the Mulligan's house today…

To, um, stop the murderer.

So I nod. I really hate lying, but maybe I've already stopped

Danny's death. Because if I hadn't been there, it would have been him chasing down Hassan, and Danny would have been in the sights of his brother, the gunman. So I make a face. "I just…"

"Can't live with yourself if you don't try. I get it…I've done it." His face grows hard. "Don't do it again. I promise, there are some consequences you can't live with."

I want to ask, but don't. Still, I apparently can't keep my youthful mouth shut. "We make changes to our timeline all the time—we just don't know what the outcome would have been. But imagine being able to save lives, to never let someone suffer—"

"You don't know what havoc you're setting in motion. A thousand tiny changes—all that carry their own ripples. It never ends…" Booker's mouth tightens. "Don't make me regret giving you the watch. I might not give it to you after all."

I can't think past the time conundrum that he already did give it to me so…okay, let's agree that he could go back and rewrite time, too, so maybe I'll just keep my mouth shut. "I won't," I say, my words true.

"Try and stay out of trouble, Stone."

The door opens and Burke walks out. "I got the report from the alarm company. Their alibi checks out."

"Jeff and Karen didn't do it," I say, my hands in my pockets. "And Swenson has an alibi."

"Yeah," Burke nods, again frowning. "Did I mention that?"

"Probably."

Booker is looking at me, and I've had enough scrutiny for today.

I'm going to pick up some ice cream and go to a party, and somehow, try and stay out of trouble.

CHAPTER 17

Eve didn't expect Rembrandt to show up, despite his words last night. If the altercation with her father was as bad as Rembrandt looked, the man should probably steer clear of Danny Mulligan for a while. A decade, maybe.

Still, the absence of Rem's black Camaro in the string of cars parked along the road in front of their Minnetonka home had her wondering why she'd spent all morning in her office, digging into the membership roles of Sigma Chi.

Oh, of course she knew. It was the look Rem gave her as he walked out the door, the words, uttered as if torn from someplace desperate inside. They shook her, really. If I lose you, I lose everything.

Talk about intense. Perhaps he meant it in a professional, she-was-working-on-his-case kind of way.

Probably.

The words drove her out of bed, however, and to the office to hound the Sigma Chi offices for the list of loyal life members from the three chapters in Minnesota. Then she spent the morning accessing the DMV records and putting faces to names in the picture from last year's event.

Tracking down the owner of the cufflinks.

She'd finally shoved the list into her pocket, glanced at the clock and high-tailed it to her parents' party.

Now, she walked up the driveway. Music blared from the back yard, Usher singing You Make Me Wanna...Clearly Asher, in charge of the boom box.

She headed around the house. The sky over the lake was a pristine blue with not a hint of last night's clouds, the lake alive with boaters and water skiers.

At the Mulligan dock, Samson was just pulling up in their ski boat, her older brother Lucas, home from Chicago for the weekend sitting copilot, a couple girls she didn't recognize sitting in the open bow.

The scent of the freshly cut grass, climbing roses and thick hosta that lined the walk suggested her mother had put her father to work. She spotted a few neighbors sitting in lawn chairs drinking cold brews.

Her father stood at the smoking grill, armed with a metal spatula and a baseball cap.

He didn't look like he'd run down a killer last night. But that was her father—he didn't bring his work home. Mom's rules.

In fact, her mother would like to live in denial that he worked for the police force at all, never mind her only daughter.

Eve bypassed the food table—piled with watermelon slices, chocolate chip cookies, brownies, and a bowl of kettle chips—and headed straight for the cooler. Pulled out a root beer, dripping and chilly.

"Hey Evie Bear."

"Dad, please."

He grinned at her, winked. Dressed in his jeans and a purple

Minnesota Vikings t-shirt, Detective Mulligan didn't quite inspire the fear he did when hunting down a murderer. She leaned into a one-armed hug from him.

"Are you okay?" She stepped back, looked him over.

"I'm fine." He turned to the grill, opened it, testing the burgers. The smell of summer billowed into the air. "Why?"

She ran her thumb down the side of the can. Glanced out toward the dock where Sams was now bobbing in the water with one ski, waiting for Lucas to hit it.

Her father closed the grill. Stood looking out at the water as Sams shouted. Lucas revved the boat and Sams popped up on one ski.

"I heard about the shooting." She didn't know why she admitted it, but...well, Rem had been so...unraveled.

She sort of thought her father might be—

"From whom?"

She drew in a breath.

"Stone, right?"

"Dad. He was just—he's worried about you. Says that maybe this Hassan guy will try and come after you."

"He should worry about himself. I wasn't the guy chasing Hassan."

"But you killed his brother."

Her father's mouth tightened.

"Do you think you're in danger?"

He looked at her now, his eyes losing the veneer of playfulness. "I'm always in danger, honey. But that's the job, right?"

His words reached in and found her heart, squeezed.

"Eve!"

The voice, coming from the porch, turned her.

Her mother stood on the deck. "Did you bring the ice cream?"

The ice cream. "Sorry!" She turned to her father. "Whoops."

"Caught up in a case?" He raised an eyebrow. "Don't worry about it. I'll run out after we eat and get some. Have a burger." He scooped one onto a bun and handed her the plate.

She wandered down to the shore, watching Sams ski by, shredding the water. Asher sat on the end of the dock and she settled down next to him with her plate.

"Hey," he said, glancing over. "I thought you were bringing your friend."

She frowned. "Really?"

He shrugged. "Maybe not. It's just…" He smiled. "I think he likes you. I saw you two kissing—"

"You need to forget you saw that, bro."

"So, you're not a thing?" He glanced over her shoulder, toward their father. "Because if you are, you should know Dad came home last night, late, ranting about Detective Stone and how he nearly got himself killed. Dad's on twenty-four hour leave for his shooting investigation and he's hot. He doesn't look like it, but—"

"No, Rembrandt and I aren't a thing." Although, really, she didn't know what they were. The man showed up at crimes scenes, and in her lab, and then at her house to kiss her…what was that?

"We just work together."

Asher smiled, his mouth a thin line. "Mmmhmm. That's why you're blushing."

"I'm not—"

Sams picked then to ski by and shower them with water. Her burger went into the lake. "Hey!" She sprang to her feet.

Asher laughed, also drenched. Sams sank into the water as he came to a halt. "What, sis, you get a little wet?"

"Just come over here and we'll see who is a little wet."

"I'm way wet, so…" He splashed her.

Perfect. Water dribbled down her neck, her T-shirt nearly see through—

Okay, so maybe she cared a little that Rem might show up.

She got up and stalked away.

"Hey!" Sams yelled. "Where are you going?"

"To buy some ice cream!" She glanced at her father, still at the grill as she marched past him. "Someday I'm going to be head of my CSI department, and you'll have to stop calling me Evie Bear."

His mouth opened, but she stalked past him, around the house toward the front entrance.

Jerks. Just because she was the only girl—

"Eve? Whoa!"

She looked up just in time for Rembrandt to dodge her.

"Rembrandt!" She staggered back a step.

"Hey." He was wearing a pair of jeans, a Journey t-shirt, his hair a little wild, unshaven and... he looked good. Wore a little smile, too, something of a smirk as he stepped back and surveyed her. "You go in the drink with your clothes on?"

"No. Sams sprayed me." She wanted to cross her arms over her shirt, but shoot, she just didn't care. She was fully clothed, wearing more than her bikini. Still, she looked bedraggled, her unruly hair in corkscrews, her clothes glued to her body.

"Want me to go drown him for you?" Rembrandt moved the bag he was carrying to his other hand, then reached up and moved a chunk of her hair out of her eyes.

Just the way he asked it, such a laughable suggestion, but one that so sided with her, she just grinned. Nodded. "Please."

"Okay. You get the getaway car ready. The keys are in the Camaro."

She laughed. "Oh, Rembrandt."

He grinned, something warm and sweet in his eyes and his

Adam's apple dipped in his throat, as if he might not be quite as confident as he let on. "Anything for you, Eve. Even jail time."

She glanced at the bag and noticed it dripping. "What's in there?"

"Ice cream. I figured I should...bring something."

"Oh, you're a life-saver. I totally forgot." She made a face. "I was at the office all morning."

"Of course you were." He set the bag down. "You work too hard."

"No, I don't."

"Yes, you do." He stepped back from her, his gaze roaming her face. "You're so amazingly smart, and someday everyone will figure that out, I promise. But you don't have to kill yourself to get there."

She stared at him, nonplussed. "How do you...how do you do that?"

"Do what?"

And she didn't want to say it because it sounded just so...so... "You just know me."

He smiled then, his eyes warm. "I...yeah. Well, I want to, I guess. And it doesn't take a detective to figure out how hard it might be to stand out in a family of overachieving brothers. And, to be the only other cop in the family. I'm sure your mother wasn't thrilled."

"No, she wasn't. In fact, she forbade us from being cops. The night my father was shot, she was so angry with him. Called him reckless and...and, well, she's told me more than once that I'm just like him."

"Oh, no, Eve, you're nothing like Danny. You're not reckless or stubborn, okay a little stubborn, maybe but—"

She swatted at him.

He dodged it. "Listen. You're a great CSI. And you're going to be at the top of your game."

"You mean I'm not already?"

His mouth opened.

"I'm playing with you, Stone." Then, and she couldn't put her finger on why, she said, quietly, "Can I tell you something?"

He nodded.

"After the coffee bombings, after you were nearly stabbed, I... well, I felt like I should have done a better job. I should have helped you find the location, maybe even the bomber—"

"Eve." He took her by the shoulders. "Stop. That was an accident—"

"What? Finding the right coffee shop?"

His expression turned a little pale. "I got lucky."

"No, you didn't. You got stabbed." She took his hands. "You could have been killed."

And for a second, the same hollow look from last night came over his face. Then, "Naw. C'mon. You've met me. I'm indestructible."

She gave him a look, but he winked at her.

There it was. The guy her father warned her about. Cocky, arrogant, and disarmingly charming.

"Besides, Eve. Don't tell me that you didn't stay up for days afterwards picking through the evidence to confirm the bomber."

Huh. Because yes, she had. "I connected him to all three bombings, just like you said. But, the one thing I'm still looking for is his designer."

Rembrandt frowned. "What?"

"The guy who designed the bombs. Ramses Vega made them, for sure, but he didn't design them. That guy is still in the wind."

The words settled on Rembrandt like an anvil and he took a breath. "Right." Then he looked at her. "Maybe we'll find him together."

Maybe. "You trust me?"

"With everything inside me," he said quietly, his eyes in hers.

And somehow, when Rem looked at her like that…she could hear her heartbeat thunder in her chest.

She'd taken a step toward him, touched his shirt. From the backyard, the radio station had turned, maybe her mother taking control. Bryan Adams was belting out a love song.

"Everything I do, I do it for you," Rem said softly, in tune with the song, his blue eyes in hers. He touched her hair. "I love it curly like this."

Her gaze fell to his mouth, nearly tasting his urgency from last night. He smelled fresh, as if he'd recently done laundry, and the smell of him, the way the summer wind moved around them, reaping the scent of freedom—

"Eve, honey, go get changed. Asher and your father will go for the ice cream."

Her mother's voice emerged from where she was coming out of the garage.

Rembrandt sucked in a breath, and Eve stilled.

"Uh oh," she said, and Rem made a face. Then, she turned.

Her mother stood in the driveway, but behind her, Danny was walking out, swinging his car keys.

Her mother's eyes widened.

Her father stopped, looked at Rembrandt and the expression on his face turned lethal.

Eve stepped away from Rem, her heart a fist. Everyone should just calm down. It wasn't like they'd caught her and Rembrandt in a clench.

Not quite yet.

"What are you doing here?"

Next to her, Rem sighed. "Listen, Danny, I just came to check on—"

"Inspector Mulligan, thanks. And if you're here for Eve, I don't think she needs you taking care of her."

"You. I came to check on you."

Danny's eyes narrowed. "Stone—"

Rembrandt flinched. She heard it too—the screech of tires, an engine being throttled. She looked at Rembrandt, whose face turned slack, and then he pushed her—really pushed her—and took off.

She hit the dirt, stunned, as Rembrandt hurtled himself toward her father.

Shots punched the air. She covered her head with her hands as a car rocketed by, peppering their yard with gunfire.

No!

Screams—probably her own—rent the air, and she couldn't look, just crawled toward the front steps, and hid herself behind them.

Dad!

Suddenly, a body hovered over her. Big, solid, his voice in her ear. "Stay down, Eve. Just stay down."

The shooting had stopped.

She trembled, her breath hiccupping as she gulped back another scream. And then the voice again. "You're okay, right?"

Not Rem's voice. Because he'd run toward her father. As if he'd known—

She looked up as the body moved away from her.

"Burke?"

He met her eyes, then raked his gaze over her body. Touched her arms. "You sure?"

"I'm okay," she said. She pushed past him to her feet.

The sight on the driveway turned her cold.

Her mother lay on the driveway, her hands pressed to her gut, writhing as blood poured between her fingers.

"Mom!"

Her father was scrambling to his feet where Rembrandt had tackled him into the grass. But Rembrandt beat him to her mother, pulled off his shirt and pushed it into her wound. "Somebody call 911!"

Her father shoved him away. "Hang on, Bets, hang on."

Rembrandt stood up, his eyes wide, breathing hard.

Then suddenly, he sprinted toward the road.

As Eve listened to Burke shout for help to the 9-1-1 operator, she spotted Rembrandt's Camaro spitting up gravel as he peeled away from the house.

CHAPTER 18

I hate time travel. I want to take Booker's stupid watch and cram it down his throat, add it to his words that thunder through my brain—you can't win against time.

Bets' blood stains my hands as I slam my foot to the floor-board of my Camaro, fishtailing around the corner off Lakeview onto Cottagewood.

These old neighborhoods are a tangle of roads, and my guess is the boys from Hassan's hood will take the easiest route back to the highway.

Back to the Phillips neighborhood.

Back into hiding.

Not if I get them first.

I saw the car. I remember the brand and make, but getting a good look at it as I took Danny to the ground and held him there has galvanized me.

But not as much as hearing Elizabeth Mulligan scream.

What sort of twisted fate version of the timeline is this? I don't remember the order of events last time—just that Asher and Danny had driven out to the nearby Cottagewood General store. Maybe

Hassan's men had staked out the house, were following them.

Why they triggered early this time I haven't a clue, except, well—and the thought is a boulder in my gut as I floor it down Cottagewood—maybe they were after me.

After all, it was me who was chasing Hassan.

I taste bile as I merge onto Minnetonka Boulevard, heading for Vine Hill.

I did this. I changed time, again.

You aren't here to save people. Changing history...you don't know what you're messing with. You don't know that the tiniest change could destroy lives.

Geez—you think?

I spot the car, heading over the Carson bay bridge as if out for a leisurely Saturday afternoon drive. Maybe they don't want to raise suspicion by speeding. Just a couple of boys from the hood, hanging out with their AR-15 semi-automatics. It's an old Buick wood paneled station wagon, just like my first timeline, and as I get closer, I spot the license plate. Memorize it.

Gotchta.

I need backup, but I don't want to lose them. Pulling my phone from my pocket, I press speed dial to Burke.

That's when the driver in the station wagon spots me. Or, I think so, because we're instantly going sixty in a forty and he's flooring it to Vinewood.

I'm running out of road. He's going to T-bone right into that intersection with Minnetonka and Vine. I punch it, coming right up on his tail.

Burke answers, but my phone has slid to the floor. "Burke, I've got him! We're on Minnetonka—"

Station wagon has hit the stop sign and taken a right, screeching out in front of an oncoming car.

The car hits the brakes, and barely misses me as I lay on the horn to alert any other oncoming cars, and follow.

My heart is outside my body. But we have a half-mile before he hits Highway 7, and I'm going to stop him before he flies out into the two-lane highway and kills people.

He's screaming down the two lane road. But I have a Camaro. Time is not going to win this round.

Hassan's shooters are going down.

They pass Deep Haven Elementary, and I know there's a curve coming up, so I get on their tail, ready to gas it.

A car in the left lane whips by, and then I floor it. I'm beside them with a clean stretch of road spooling out ahead of me.

I don't want to bang up the Camaro. But what choice do I have? The highway appears ahead of me, cars stopped at the light, and to the right, I spot a line of vehicles merging into the side road, coming out of a church.

A wedding. That fact tickles something deep in my brain, but I don't have time, because the wagon isn't slowing down, and someone is going to die.

It might be me. But right now, all I'm thinking about is Eve, and the fact that losing her mother might be the one thing she doesn't recover from.

And I don't care what Booker, or my Dad said.

I can't be here and not try. I love Eve enough to keep her from walking through all that pain of waiting for justice.

It's all I have to give her, after everything I did to her—or will do to her.

I yank the wheel to the right and hit the gas, slamming into the front of the station wagon. I brace myself and stay the course.

We are careening for the ditch. A car pulls out fifty feet in front of us.

I hit the brakes.

The force throws me forward—and I thank Eve for her relentless pursuit to make me a better, safer, man, because instinct has hooked me into my seatbelt as the two of us—the wagon and the Camaro—spin.

The wagon jerks around, taking me with it. The force rips me free of the pavement and my car takes to the air.

We—my car and I—land, roll and I'm conscious for most of it. When we shudder to a stop, we are wheels side down.

I'm gulping breaths, my heart nowhere near my body. But I'm alive.

My Camaro, not so much. The car is wheezing, still trying to breathe, wedged against a tree in the ditch.

Sorry, sweetheart.

Sirens scream in the background.

I press my hands to my chest, and yes, I am intact, although I'll be bruised by the belt. Freeing myself, I try the door—yeah, that's not happening. The roof is dented, but the passenger door opens, and I kick it wider. I dive out, onto all fours, crawling.

"Are you okay?"

The voice makes me look up, and for a second, I'm not sure where I am. Because the man is sturdy, with military short, gray-brown hair, and blue eyes, and he's wearing a concern on his face that I recognize from before.

"Art?"

He frowns and looks over his shoulder. "Sheila! He's bleeding! Bring a towel."

I'm bleeding? "Not my blood," I manage and push past him, my eyes sweeping the area. "Get back in your car." I climb to the road, and continue to search for the station wagon.

It's in the ditch on the other side of the road, on its side, the driver's side up. And, it too, is smoking.

The sirens are louder, now, but I'm ignoring them, my body running hot as I circle the wagon.

The front windshield is destroyed and even from here I see that the passenger, the shooter, now crumpled half-out of the broken glass, isn't going to stand trial.

His driver is in rough shape, too, crumpled on top of his body.

I bend over, grab my knees, and lose it. And not because of the gruesome sight.

But, maybe, because this time, I won. That fact leaves me shaken, undone and, to be honest, terrified.

Because I know time is a sore loser.

I glance at Art and Shelia who just stare at me. Sheila is holding a towel.

The sirens have stopped at the crash, and I'm wiping my mouth as an officer runs down to me. "Sir—are you okay?"

He's a big man and looks vaguely familiar and it's then I notice his name. Williams.

Big Jimmy Williams, now working for the Excelsior department. I have the desperate urge to tell him not to change precincts. Or better, retire now.

"Detective Rembrandt Stone. These men are shooters in a nearby drive-by."

"Over at the Mulligan's place?"

I am nearly weak with relief. So, they already know. "How's Bets?"

He speaks into his radio, asking for an update. "They're on their way to the HCMC Trauma Center."

I climb up the bank, back onto the road.

The Camaro has died, not a hint of life, the body destroyed, but I don't have time to mourn.

I need a ride.

I'm searching, and my gaze lands on a red Toyota Camry, still parked in the middle of the road, blocking traffic on both sides.

Art has returned to his car, and is sitting at the wheel, his door open, one leg out as if he's not sure what to do.

I have a job for him.

It doesn't take much for Art and Sheila to agree to take me downtown to the Hennepin County Medical Center. They take one look at the blood on my hands, on my bare chest—yes, I took off my Journey shirt to staunch Bets' wounds—and tell me to climb in.

I don't wait to give a report. I have no doubt Burke, or Booker, or even Williams will track me down.

"You're hurt," Sheila says, and it's now I realize I'm a little scuffed up, as well as half-naked.

"Here." Art shucks off his suit jacket. "Take this."

I want to argue but I did save their lives. "Thanks."

"What happened back there, son?" Art says, and glances at me through the rear-view mirror.

Time is laughing at me. We're all in this tangle of events, enmeshed, regardless of how it spools out.

"Drive by shooter. I'm a cop."

"A shooting? Out here, in Minnetonka?" Sheila is wearing a lavender dress, and I am wondering if it's the one she died in, in the previous version of her timeline.

"Retaliation shooting for something that went down last night."

"Oh my. This is why we moved to Stillwater," Sheila says. "We used to live in this cute house on Webster Avenue, just a few miles up the road. But Art found the perfect Tudor in Stillwater, and I thought...what if we changed our lives? Found something safer, and simpler. Brought our daughter up in a small town?" She touches Art's shoulder. "We started late. Our daughter is only seven. But we have no complaints."

I must be shaken up more than I realize because my throat is thickening, my eyes burning.

I want my life back. But in my gut, I know it's gone. All of it.

My sick feeling is that Ashley is not coming back and I have to figure out how to live with what remains.

Our mistakes, our tragedies, our suffering makes us better, stronger, more compassionate people. And those are lessons we learn by going through the pain, not around it.

I swallow, a fist in my chest because I know what awaits me, if I ever get back there. But at least maybe now I can prepare for it.

Be a better Rembrandt the second time around.

They let me off at the emergency entrance. "Thanks," I say, and then Art looks at me, frowns. "Wait. Did we meet before? Maybe a month ago? You came to visit me?"

Sheila looks at me. "You're the guy with the watch."

"Not anymore," I say. Because as soon as I find Booker, I'm giving it back.

He can keep his time travel.

I thank them and walk to the reception area. My appearance raises the eyebrows of a few nurses and I again explain the blood isn't mine. I show my badge and ask about Elizabeth Mulligan.

She's in surgery, her family is gathered in the second floor CCU waiting room.

I know the way, having been this route so many years ago.

The first time, Asher was in surgery—Danny already pronounced—and I found Eve standing at the window, staring out into the night as fireworks shot over the river.

Our relationship found its footing that night as worry turned into grief. As she sat in the chairs and dissolved, my arms around her.

Her mother had Samson and Lucas.

Eve had me. And sure, we had our drama after that night, mostly because of Eve's obsession to find her father and brother's killers. But this time around, that's not happening.

This time around it's not her father. Not her brother.

Oh, Bets, I'm so sorry.

I get off the elevator and head down the hall, bracing myself for what I already know.

Please—and maybe God and I haven't been exactly talking over the past decade, but I don't know anyone else to ask. So, please, God, let Bets be alive.

The Mulligan family is standing in a huddle, talking to a doctor when I arrive. Danny is covered in blood, although his hands are washed, and Asher appears drawn, yet very much alive. Samson stands wide-legged, his arms folded over his chest and Lucas's lawyer's mouth is pinched, listening as the doctor gives them the news.

I am not close enough to hear, but I clench my jaw and look at Eve.

She's standing just behind Sams. And behind her stands Burke, his hands on her shoulders.

Then she covers her face with her hands, her body shuddering and I know. I need to be there, to hold her—

She turns into Burke's embrace, and I'm stunned, my gait slowing.

Then, Danny looks up and sees me.

His expression confuses me. Not quite hatred, not quite acceptance. Confusion, maybe.

I swallow hard as the doctor leaves them, and approach. "I'm so sorry—"

"How did you know?" Danny's eyes are fierce, hard in mine. "How did you know it was a drive by shooting?"

I open my mouth, close it. "I didn't. I just—I heard the car, and I thought of Hassan and—"

"Stone." Danny takes a shaky breath. Swallows. "Thank you."

I am blinking at him, words dropping away. What?

His jaw is tight, as if he's fighting emotion, or saying more.

My mouth is dry, and I need a drink. Water. I need water. "I'm sorry I couldn't protect Bets. I should have—"

Danny shakes his head. "It's not your fault."

But, see, it is.

"How is she?"

"Serious. They're taking her into surgery now. But..." He glances at Sams, at Asher. "But it could have been Asher. Or me."

I say nothing.

"Rembrandt! Are you okay?"

Eve has come up to me, taking in my bloody chest and I'm aware that I'm bare-chested under the jacket.

"I'm okay." I look at Danny. "I got the shooters."

Danny considers me, his eyes glassy, and nods. "Thank you, son."

Son. Huh.

Burke is giving me a look over the top of Eve's head. "I got your call. So, did you total the Camaro?"

I grimace.

"You should sit down," Eve says and pulls me over to one of the green chairs lining the hallway.

"I'll see if I can rustle you up a shirt." Burke walks down the hall.

Eve checks me over, not like you think, but in a clinical, CSI kind of way, examining my hands, the scrapes on my body. "You have a bruise across your chest."

"Seatbelt."

"Well, at least you're not an idiot."

That could be seriously debated, but I'm not going to argue.

She slides onto a chair next to me. Danny has walked to the window, Samson next to him.

Asher sits down beside Eve. "Last time we were here, you were waiting for Rembrandt."

I look over at Eve. Really? She waited in the chairs for me?

She lifts a shoulder at me.

How I love this woman. And, I don't care what has happened in our future, I'm not letting her go.

"Oh, Rem, by the way—you should know this. I got the list of Sigma Chi members. The loyal lifers who were at the annual party." She leans up—she's still wearing her shorts, although her shirt is dry—and pulls a piece of paper from her back pocket. It's a little soggy as I unfold it.

I scan the list, expecting one name.

"Jeff Holmes isn't on this list."

"He's not a loyal life Sig. He dropped his membership shortly after graduation."

My gaze goes down the list. And stops. "Robert Swenson."

"Yeah. I haven't checked it yet, but it might be the credit card guy."

"Her softball coach."

Burke is carrying a t-shirt in his hand, a tag dangling from the arm. He might have picked it up in the gift shop. I stand and meet him. "What did you say was Robert Swenson's alibi?"

"Softball practice," he tosses me the shirt. It's black and has a red cancer-society heart in the center.

I shrug off the jacket and pull it over my head. It's a little tight, but it works. "C'mon. We have a softball tournament to attend. And, you're driving."

I turn, and look at Eve, then Danny, and back to Eve. "I'll be back."

CHAPTER 19

The sun is a simmering ball against the horizon, casting looming shadows into the softball multi-plex located in St. Louis park. All four baseball diamonds are active with softball and baseball teams, the players sweltering under the hot afternoon sun. The park is packed, players smacking balls on the nearby tennis courts, smoke rolling off barbeques, families playing Frisbee and dogs barking.

Burke parks us in a lot near the softball fields, and we get out. The lot is full, but near the entrance we pass a maroon caravan with a Hornets sticker on the back mirror. I peek inside and see a car seat buckled into one of the back bucket seats.

Next to it is a sweet looking Corvette I salivate over a bit.

Oh, my poor Camaro.

I glance in the Corvette's window, too, and spot a mesh bag of softball supplies in the back—helmets, gloves, balls—crammed into the back.

We head out behind the backstops and I'm searching for the uniforms of the Edina Hornets. I spot the team on the field, wearing green and gold.

Their fans are packed into a tiny string of bleachers, cheering. Burke and I wander over and stand at the fence. I spot who I think is Robert Swenson—my memory after twenty-plus years is dim— but he glances over and sees Burke. Nods.

The guy with the blonde hair, slight paunch, and balding is not quite the Casanova I expected him to be. He's wearing a green hornets t-shirt, a cap and a pair of shorts, and is yelling at the short-stop to move over.

"There's his wife," Burke says and points to a woman sitting on the end of the bleachers, first row. Petite, blonde hair tied back in the messy buns of the '90s, she's holding a fat toddler on her lap. She's wearing a hat and dark sunglasses. She cheers as a batter steps up to the plate.

"I'm going to have a chat with her. Keep an eye on Robert." I head over to the bleachers. Burke doesn't move because he knows what I'm doing.

In fact, it clicks in, just now, that he must have been at the Mulligans when the shots were fired. Huh. Maybe he followed me. We'll get to the bottom of that later. For now, I'm just having a casual conversation with Angie.

It's a good thing I stopped in the bathroom to wash my hands before we left because now I look just like a regular guy watching the game.

There's a little space on the end of the row, so I gesture to it and ask to sit down.

She nods and I settle in.

"Go Hornets!" she yells and it's the perfect opening.

"You have a player on the team?"

She looks at me. She's pretty. Late twenties. A little weariness around the eyes, maybe. "No. My husband is the coach. But I used to play, so I can't stop myself. I sort of want to get out there."

"What position?"

"Short stop." She looks at me. "For the Hopkins Lions."

The hitter smacks the ball high out to right field, and it's easily nabbed.

"Did your husband play baseball?"

"Yep. We were high school sweethearts."

The next batter comes up. She helps Junior clap.

"Cute. How old is he?"

"Fourteen months." She gives him a kiss. "Samuel Ezekiel Swenson. Long awaited child." She looks at me. "We've been married seven years, so Samuel is a real gift."

She leaves out the details, but I can guess. Infertility struggles probably, given the delay.

The batter hits a line drive through the shortstop's legs and the crowd groans at the base hit.

"Gretta would have caught that," says someone nearby and beside me, Angie stiffens.

"Gretta?" I keep my voice easy.

"Our short stop. She was...well, she, uh, she passed away." She looks straight ahead, and swallows. "Yesterday."

"I'm sorry."

"Mmmhmm. C'mon, Hornets!" She glances at me, cuts her voice down. "She was a little troubled. Ran away from home. Robert was trying to help her. He met with her once in a while to talk."

I think she sees Burke standing a few feet away because she stills, then glances at me. "Are you with him?"

I nod slowly. "But we're just having a friendly chat. I was a little curious, however, about something."

She looks back at the game. It's two-and three, full count. The crowd is cheering. "Who are you?"

"My name is Rembrandt Stone. I'm a detective." I slide out

my ID, let her have a quick glance, then tuck it away.

"What do you want?"

"Just a couple quick answers to a couple quick questions."

She doesn't respond so I dive in. "What's your husband driving these days?"

She looks at me, one brow down. "A Corvette."

"Except on practice days, I'll bet, huh? Because he has to take the caravan to the field to haul equipment."

Her mouth tightens. "Yeah, I suppose."

"Hard to get the car seat in a Corvette."

She looks at me and frowns. "Mmmhmm."

My mind is pinging back to Teresa's comment about the cars outside. Nothing out of the ordinary.

"Strike three!" The words from the umpire turn my gaze back to the field. And it's now that I see Robert off to the side talking with a man.

No, talking with Jeff Holmes.

What is he doing here?

I get up and glance at Burke. Because Jeff has put his hand on Robert's chest, pushing him. A father never stops caring.

Especially a father obsessed, grieving and desperate for justice. I'm familiar with the type, so, oh boy. "Burke—"

"Yep," he says and we take off around the back of the dugout toward the altercation.

Someone screams when Jeff grabs one of the bats lodged into the fencing. His voice raises. "I'll kill you for what you did to her!"

Robert has picked up a bat too and the two are facing off. "I didn't kill her!"

"You raped her!" Jeff takes a swing at Robert, who dodges.

"I didn't!" He backs up, sweating. Jeff takes two quick steps toward him.

"Jeff! Stop!" I shout, but he's beyond hearing. Really, I don't blame him. He takes another swing at Robert who meets his bat with a resounding clang that rattles even my bones.

The vibration makes him drop the bat and he staggers back, his hands up.

"Stop—"

"She was a kid. Just a kid, and you—I don't care if she agreed—you got into her head. You—" Jeff drops a description that is apt but probably has the mothers in the stands gasping.

Not me. This scum deserves whatever Jeff dishes out.

But I can't let Jeff go down for murder, so— "Jeff! Let us handle it!"

He ignores me and swings again.

This time, as he back peddles, Robert trips.

He's a sitting duck. Well, lying I guess. He rolls over and is crawling across the ground when Jeff runs him down. Grabs his collar, raises the bat.

He's going to break ribs—or, if he hits his head, Robert really is dead.

I'm just three steps away, so of course I launch myself at Jeff.

The man goes down under me. But let's not forget he's a bit of a loose cannon and wasn't afraid to hurt me before. He roars and slams an elbow into my side. It bulls-eyes on the still-healing stab wound, and I submit to an inner howl. But I grit my teeth, grab his arm and lay on him. "Stay down!"

No murder in front of the kiddos, pal.

"He didn't do it!" Angie has run up behind us, and she's crying, holding her baby, standing away from both men, but shouting over and over. "He didn't do it!"

And he didn't. Because the crime has already formed in my head.

Robert didn't kill Gretta.

Angie did.

Or at least she was there.

Nothing out of the ordinary. Maybe a caravan, or a couple sedans, Teresa said.

Burke is there, again, with cuffs and I roll off Jeff to let my partner subdue him.

I'm breathing hard, and in a little pain as I glance at Angie. She might have run to his defense, but there is nothing of rescue in her expression now. She's staring at Robert in a way that looks like she'd like to pick up the bat, have a go at him.

"You were the one at Lulu's yesterday morning," I say, my voice quiet. "You went to talk to Gretta,"

Angie looks at me. "Of course I did. I thought maybe—"

"You could talk her into having an abortion."

She took in a breath. "She was already thinking it—I know it. She was at that clinic. I picked her up and we argued. I gave her some money and I told her we'd pay for it, but she was angry and she got out and ran—" She looks at Robert. "You did this. You stole our lives from us."

Robert is still breathing hard, still on the ground and I wouldn't mind picking up the bat, either. "How did you know?" he asks Angie.

A wife knows, is what Eve would say. I can hear her voice, and suddenly long to get back to her.

Please, don't die, Bets. I still can't believe I screwed up that badly.

Angie's voice, so full of vitriol shakes me back to the now. "She called me, Robert. She told me everything."

"I tried to take care of it. I tried to talk to her—"

"You tried to strangle her," Burke says to Robert. "That's where she got the bruises. You scared her. And that's why she called Angie. And then, she called her mother."

Poor Karen. If she'd only waited a few more minutes. She'd gone looking for Gretta, but her daughter was trapped in Angie's caravan, having an argument outside the clinic.

The same caravan Robert drove to the game the day Jeff had it out with him. After his deal. Where he was wearing his cuff links, all cocky, like he was some hotshot, Jeff had said.

Just to confirm my racing deductions—"Jeff, when you and Robert had that fight—was he driving the caravan?"

Jeff frowns, looks at Robert. "Yeah."

"You grabbed his shirt, didn't you? Maybe his sleeve?"

Jeff lifts a shoulder, then nods.

"Robert, did you lose a cuff link?"

His eyes are widening. "How did you—"

"It fell out at Lulu's, when your wife got out to chase Gretta."

Angie is crying now. "She was running, and I was desperate, so I did chase her, but then, Sammy was crying, and I couldn't leave him, and I shouted at her that we weren't finished." She puts her hand over her mouth, her eyes widening. "She looked back at me and—"

"You saw her trip. Saw her hit her head."

Angie stiffens. "I didn't know she was that hurt. She screamed and fell and I...I got back in the caravan and drove home. If I'd known she was dying..." She tightens her jaw, and her eyes spark. "She was a tramp who shouldn't have my husband's child."

Jeff makes a sound, something of a keening, but I get it.

It's the sound of despair, and somewhere inside me, it connects with the subconscious memory of losing Ashley.

I'm broken for him.

"I'll call Booker and have him send a squad car," I say to Burke.

197

I give Angie a look. "You stay here."

Then I walk over to Robert and help him up from the grass.

"Thanks," he says.

I don't have cuffs, but Booker will.

For a second, I wonder what I'll say to my old boss, the instigator of this mess. Look him in the eye and say enough? Because Jeff is weeping, and so resembles a man I saw in the mirror two days ago.

I can't take any more loss.

Maybe justice isn't enough.

But as Jeff looks up, and takes a breath, I realize...maybe it's a start.

You spend all your time trying to figure out if you could have done something different, rewriting your responses, imagining a different outcome. At least now they know.

"You're under arrest for the attempted murder of Gretta Holmes."

"Wait—" Robert says.

"Shut your mouth and listen. You have the right to remain silent—"

But that's all I get out because I hear the train. The rumble of the future reaching out to grab me.

No, oh no, I need to get back to Eve. To fireworks and everything we have before us.

This time, we're going to make it.

I look over at Burke, then let go of Robert and head over to the chain link fence and hold on. The wind surges around me, the world is dropping away.

I close my eyes and fight a scream deep in my core.

Because I haven't a clue what I might find waiting on the other side.

Chapter 20

I hear screaming—and it could be me—as time blinks me back to reality. Or my new reality. Present day timeline. Whatever you want to call it.

Thankfully, I find myself in the conference room again, and on instinct, I catch myself with my hands to break my fall. I'm listening to my heartbeat, but shrieks erupt from the hallway.

And then I remember—

My Porsche. The explosion. Burke!

I scramble to my feet, then to the door.

The screaming has stopped, and out in the bullpen, guys sit at their desks, no one panicking at a man burning to death on the street. "Who's screaming?" I say and someone I don't recognize looks up and frowns at me.

Huh. But I know I heard it—I turn back to the conference room and head to the window, glancing at the board on the way.

Wait.

The board is crammed with photos of victims of the Jackson killer.

He's been busy in my jump back to the present, and a hot ball of horror forms in my gut. Over a dozen more victims, from my quick count.

He's been busy because I did something.

The scream rises again, sharp and fast and I run to the window.

No burning Porsche. But across the street where used to be an empty lot is a...park? Kids are playing on swings, climbing the jungle gym, running around the space.

Screaming.

I stare at the activity a long moment, caught suddenly in a fading distant memory of my seven-year-old, her blonde hair flipping behind her as she digs into a swing on the set I built for her...less than a week ago. My chest tightens.

Maybe she's back.

Please...

Although with the cases on the board, something inside me says no. Still, to confirm, I turn and take a look at my desk.

It's clean. The files hanging in their own partitions in a long file box that sits parallel to a real desk. And on the front I see a nameplate.

Captain Stone.

What? So apparently, I haven't completely screwed up my life. I sort through the files, looking for anything familiar.

Ashley's folder is gone.

Gretta's is too, so maybe—

"Hey Captain, I got those reports you were looking for." The knock at the door lifts my head and I don't recognize the man who strolls in. He's young, mid-twenties, dark hair queued back in a man bun, and he wears a suit jacket over a t-shirt, a pair of jeans and Cons.

I'm looking at a younger version of myself, and for a second, I wonder if maybe I've cloned myself, sent it to the future—no, that's the stuff of sci-fi novels. Be real, Rem.

I notice the name on his badge. Kincaid.

He hands me the file and I look at it. "Remind me...?"

"It's the first Jackson murder." He gives me a puzzled look. "You asked the CSI Director to revisit the DNA samples found under her fingernails?"

"Right." I haven't a clue what he's talking about, of course. "Thanks."

I set the file on my desk, and Kincaid just stands there, looking at me. "Um—"

"We're sparring today, right? After work?" He looks at his watch.

Me too, but mine has stopped working, of course. "We are?"

He frowns. "You said you'd show me that counter punch move you do."

I'd love to know what that is, too. Maybe I can Google it.

"Yeah, sure." I say. "I'll see you then."

"Super."

From the hallway, someone stops at the door and sticks their head into my office. "Hey, Zeke! Some of the guys are getting pizza. You want some?"

"Sure," The man named Kincaid says. Zeke Kincaid.

"Nice. I'll tell Burke you're in." The officer nods and heads away, but the name sends an arrow of relief through me. Burke is still here.

He hasn't been burned alive.

"Let me know if you need anything else, boss," Zeke says.

How about a sit-rep on my life? But I don't say that as I let Zeke walk away.

So, the Jackson killer is still at large, and I walk to the board and do the math. Thirty-seven total. That's fourteen new names.

What have I done?

I focus back on the facts. Apparently, I'm hunting down a lead on victim number one. Who wasn't Gretta Holmes.

I'm a little curious, so I return to my computer and wiggle the mouse. It's locked, and I put in my password, Ashley.

It doesn't work and I'm a little surprised because even in my last timeline, the one of her murder, I used it. I try Eve.

Nothing.

A tiny sweat breaks out down my back because I haven't a clue, not one, of what else I'd use.

Mulligan. Nope.

I'm drumming my fingers on my desk and my gaze falls on a picture of me and Mikey, grease-covered and grinning. I'm about ten.

Michelangelo.

The screen opens. Interesting.

I get into our criminal files and search Robert Swenson's name. The results take a swipe out of me. He served a dime for attempted murder and three counts of sexual assault—the report names two other women besides Gretta. Was paroled ten years ago, put on the sexual predator list, and was caught with a fourteen-year-old girl a couple years later. He's currently in Stillwater, chewing up a twenty-year sentence.

There's also a brief mention of Angie. She wasn't charged with Gretta's death, in return for her testimony against Robert. I do the math and guess her son would be in mid-twenties by now. I hope she moved on and found someone who wouldn't betray her, hope little Samuel found a good man to raise him.

"Oh, I'm glad you're here."

The voice slides through me like honey. I look up and for a second, I can't breathe.

Eve stands in the doorway, her hair short—really short, almost shorn to her head, but still fluffy and pretty. She's wearing a pair of linen pants, a sleeveless shirt and sandals. She doesn't look like she's coming from work, but maybe. A satchel hangs from her shoulder, and she's holding a paper bag.

A lunch bag. A wild hope shoots through me that it's my lunch, and she's here to bring it to me, and we're that couple now, that can't go a half-day without seeing each other.

"Eve," I say, and come around the desk. "You look...really nice." I come up to her, too eager, maybe, but she is smiling so warmly, I can't help myself.

I reach for her.

She laughs and puts out her hand to my chest. "Rembrandt? Seriously? You want him to kill you?"

Him? I stop, and it's then I spot a ring on her finger.

Not my ring.

A wave of despair sweeps through me.

It was probably too much to hope, but...and then it hits me.

Silas. I'm so going to murder him. "Sorry," I mutter. I'm new here, so I'm not quite ready to commit a felony until I know all the facts.

Eve takes a step away, as if reinforcing her words. "I was going through some old boxes, and I found this. I thought I'd drop it off for you." She holds out the bag. Offers a tight smile.

I take it and open it.

My journey concert shirt. The image of Bets, bleeding on the ground, slashes through my mind. I must go pale because Eve touches my arm. "You probably saved her life that night."

I swallow hard, my eyes burn and I blink fast as I look at Eve. "You're mom—she's—"

"She says hi, and that she missed you at Dad's memorial

203

birthday last night. But I get it. We're so close to catching this guy—" Her gaze moves past me to the board. "My office sent over the DNA test you ordered. Did you get it?"

Her office. So, she's still on the job. Another sweet rush of relief. "I did."

"You'll get him, Rem. No one is as good as you."

This time her smile is genuine, and in it I see fragments of our past.

So I did mean something to her, once upon a time.

And then the other part of her sentence pings inside me.

Danny's memorial birthday party.

No...

But Eve doesn't look quite so haunted, quite so undone, so maybe I did fix something.

"Eve, Babe. What are you doing here?"

She turns to the voice, one that I know so well, and smiles.

It's a sucker punch right to my sternum, because not only do I know that voice, but I also know the smile Eve flashes.

That smile is love. Acceptance. Knowing and being known.

That's the smile of intimacy. And she's giving it to Andrew Burke.

The screaming is back in my head as Burke walks over to the woman I love and kisses her, like it's as natural as breathing.

I, however, can't breathe, as I stare at Burke. He's wearing a uniform, as if he's back on patrol, but there's something easier about him.

As if he's not quite so tightly wound.

He lets her go. "I'm just off shift. You ready?"

She nods. "Daphne is in the car. We just got back from the library. She has a slew of books she thinks she's going to read in a week." She laughs and then glances at me. "Thirteen year olds—she's exactly the right age to believe in Prince Charming and happily ever after."

Burke laughs, and takes her hand. Then he turns to me.

His smile vanishes and a crisp air blows between us. "Boss," he says, as if saying hello. Or goodbye. Or stay out of my way. I'm not exactly sure because my radar has short circuited.

The entire right side of Burke's face is distorted—a rumpled, shiny, ages old burn scar. It runs down the side of his face, into his neck and disappears under his uniform.

I'm a good liar, yes, but not so good that I can tear my gaze away quickly. I linger a moment, then find my footing and meet his eyes.

A chill slices through me because deep inside his gaze I catch a glimpse of something I've never before seen in Burke.

Hate.

I swallow, and nod. "Officer Burke," I say in quiet, pained dismissal.

He takes Eve's hand and they walk to the door.

I take hold of the frame of my door.

An officer walks by me, holding a stack of pizza boxes.

I could retch. Instead, I go to my desk, find my keys, grab my suit coat—apparently, I'm back to that—and head out to the parking lot.

After everything I've been through, I don't know why I want to fall to my knees and weep at the sight of my Porsche. Maybe because she's still intact, the one thing in my world that hasn't changed. In fact, she's clean and beautiful under the warm June air. I get in and pull out, cranking the radio to drown out the cacophony of voices inside.

Eve is married to Burke.

Burke's been seriously injured.

He's no longer my partner.

Danny is dead.

And Ashley…I sit at the light, the realization like tar through me.

Ashely wasn't murdered by the Jackson killer.

Ashley has never existed.

I turn the volume higher and shake my head to the words of the Kansas song, Carry on Wayward Son, mocking me. Somewhere in the lyrics it promises peace, when I'm done.

Not a chance.

I'm going to gamble big and hope that I still had the smarts to buy the 1930s craftsman on Washburn, just a stone's throw from Lake Calhoun.

I pull into the driveway. It's not that different. Still painted its former gray, and minus Eve's landscaping. I get out and try my key.

It works and I have weak legs as I walk inside.

I have done the math, figured out that Eve has not been here to decorate, but my chest still hollows at the starkness of my bachelor pad. A lot of over-sized leather furniture in the family room, a massive flat screen on the wall (I don't hate that), and some shots of me on a boat, holding a prize fish.

There's a picture of me and Booker, his arm over my shoulder as I hold up my captain's badge.

Booker. He must be still gone, because I have the watch, right?

I slide off my shoes and go into my kitchen. The bottle of Macallan's is gone, and when I open my fridge, I'm shaken by the amount of rabbit food. Vegetables, fruit, and a few packages of tofu.

You've gotta be kidding. I've turned Vegan. And, not one beer. Not that I need a drink this early, but…yeah, I'm gonna look.

My former liquor cabinet is filled with containers of powdered protein.

Fine.

I make a shake and head to my office.

I can fix this. I have to fix this.

The leather chair Eve gave me when I retired from the force is gone, but the office is clean, the desk bigger and on the shelf behind it, my first and only book, The Last Year. A memoir about my cases.

But beside those are a number of awards. Investigative commendations.

So, I'm not a complete disaster. And I'm healthy.

And I'm the boss.

But I don't have Eve. Or Ashley.

This is not a world I can live in.

I sit down at the computer and wiggle the mouse. The lock screen comes on, and since I'm not that original, I enter in the same password from work.

Bingo.

Then I start digging.

Because I remember a fire, long, long ago, one that happened weeks after Danny and Asher's death while Burke and I were tracking down the shooters. We arrived on the scene late, the house an inferno.

Two children were trapped inside.

It took something out of Burke to watch it burn, and he'd tried to enter the house. We fought, I won, and we watched the fire burn from across the street.

I find the article of the fire, buried in decades of fires in the Phillips neighborhood, and scan it.

Two officers injured in the fire. One died—and fate is cruel when I realize it's Danny.

And it's all my fault. No, really it is. Because who else can change time?

Footsteps on my front porch make me look up. Someone is at the door, fiddling with the lock.

My instincts have me on my feet and out into the hallway, and when it opens, I grab the man and push him up to the wall.

"Hey! What—Rembrandt. Sheesh, it's me!"

The guy is tall, decently built, and is wearing a t-shirt under a suitcoat. Brownish red hair, a little long, and in his mid-thirties. He puts his hands up. "Step back, bro."

I know I recognize him, I just can't—wait. "Asher?"

"Who did you expect, Santa?" He puts his hands down. "You need to stop working out so hard. You're starting to look like the Rambo guy you love."

I love Rambo?

Asher pushes past me. "I came home to grab an HDMI cable. Wouldn't you know it? The children we hired at MinneHack think everything happens over Bluetooth."

He takes the stairs and I watch him go. Then, because I can't stop, I follow him.

He's in Ashley's room. Except the walls aren't pink. The stuffed animals are gone and it's been fashioned into a sort of computer hub, with multiple monitors on a standing desk and rows and rows of CPU units, all humming. Asher is searching through a big drawer, pulling out cables.

"What is going on?"

He glances over his shoulder. "Sorry. I know you've got that big date coming up tonight. I'll try not to bother you." He winks.

Date? Big date? I'm more than a little horrified.

Asher grabs the cable and pushes past me. "By the way, forget what I said about Shelby. She's great. I'm sure you two will live happily ever after. Just give me a sixty day notice before you kick me out, okay?" He goes down the stairs.

Shelby? The woman from dispatch that Burke dated, eons ago?

I sink down on the top of the stairs, hearing an echo from a past I'd like to grab back. Or maybe you just stay here and try and live with your new reality.

My answer is the same.

Not a chance.

The epic series continues with Rembrandt Stone in two months.
Check out a sneak peek of book three. Join us in June for the
next installment.

THE TRUE LIES
OF REMBRANDT STONE

STICKS AND STONE

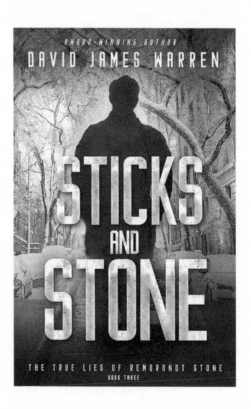

STICKS AND STONE
CHAPTER 1 - SNEAK PEAK

The pieces of two lives sit in my brain like they should fit together, but no matter how hard I press, I can't get them to line up.

My life is broken into fragments that no longer match.

All I know is that you can't escape your past, no matter how you try.

And believe me, I've tried.

I'm standing on the muddy shoreline in the shadow of the Stone Arch bridge on the east bank of the Mississippi river. The morning sun is low, just brimming the horizon, gilding the water a deep, fire-orange, and turning the skyline of Minneapolis a brilliant gold. I'm watching my crime scene investigators tape off a wooded area of the historic Main Street Park just off Anthony and Main.

A woman's naked body is covered, awaiting the CSI director—my former wife, although she has no memory of that—and the coroner is on his way.

I am nursing my second cup of coffee, the first one downed

this morning at o-dark hundred as I crawled out of bed to the text of my assistant, Inspector Zeke Kincaid.

My head is fuzzy because, as I said, I'm trying to fit together pieces that aren't made for this puzzle.

This puzzle belongs to Rembrandt Stone, Bureau Chief Inspector for the Minneapolis Police Department and head of the task force overseeing the Jackson serial killings.

I am Rembrandt Stone, former Investigator turned failed novelist, father to a seven-year-old daughter, gone missing in time, husband to a wife who can't remember being married to him, and the owner of a time-traveling watch.

This is a lifetime I haven't yet lived, and although the pieces are starting to form, I'm going to need a lot more coffee.

And help.

Here's what I know—and you'd better write this down because I'm getting some of my facts mixed up as time folds upon itself.

Four days ago, while I was celebrating my daughter's seventh birthday, with my beautiful wife Eve, my former boss, Police Chief John Booker gave me his old broken watch—bequeathed to me after his death—and a file box of my old cold cases.

Three days ago, I took said watch to a repairman who told me it was working just fine. Maybe, because as I was looking over my cold cases—specifically the first one involving the bombing of three coffee shops over twenty years ago—I inadvertently wound the watch.

And ended up at the scene of the first bombing.

I know what you're thinking—me too. Maybe I'd had too much Macallan's for a night cap. But stay with me—I solved those bombings and prevented the third. And woke up in a new reality. One where my wife stood on my doorstep and handed me divorce papers.

One where Ashley had been murdered, two years before.

One I desperately needed to escape.

So, two days ago, I sought out the watchmaker, and he—and his daughter—suggested that I'd overwritten the events of my previous timeline.

Intending to re-write them yet again, yesterday, I traveled back to my second cold case, one involving a young woman murdered near a diner. I'll be honest—my goal wasn't to solve her crime, but to stop another…the drive by shooting deaths of Eve's father and brother.

Really, it's not that hard to change history when you know the time and place history is going to happen. Danny and Asher lived. More on that later.

Yesterday, when I returned to this reality, I found Eve married to my partner, Burke.

Former partner Burke. I'm still figuring out that glitch.

And, worse, Ashley doesn't exist. Has never existed.

Are you keeping up?

Maybe we should simply rewind time to yesterday when I arrived back—or should I say forward?—to now and discovered that my life wasn't in tatters.

I'm not a drunk, I'm not on the verge of divorce, my daughter isn't among the victims, strangled in her pajamas, torn from our lives as she slept in her upstairs bedroom.

On the contrary, I'm successful. Published.

And I still have my Porsche.

I have a good life.

It's just not a life I want.

My house is the same—the 1930s craftsman, off Drew Avenue, close enough to the lakes for us—me—to feel like we're near a park, but with the skyline just a stone's throw away.

It's not been remodeled, and that's probably because I no longer have Eve in my ear drawing out her dreams on graph paper. Inside, my office bookcase is filled with a row of best-sellers, my name on the spine, so now I know what I do on my nights off.

I share the house with Asher Mulligan—I nearly tackled him as he came into the house, mostly because I didn't recognize him, having never known Asher as an adult. Because, you know, he died. Until he didn't.

Oh boy.

He is apparently my roommate, a white-hat hacker and someone with whom I'm friendly, if not close.

I don't know who I'm close to, really, because the only two people in my life I'd put in that category have each other now.

Eve, my wife, and Burke.

Andrew Burke, my former partner. Who now hates me, and bears a terrible burn scar across his face. I'm going to get to the bottom of that.

My office is still a conference room, but now, instead of twenty-three horrific murders, thirty-eight cases line the board.

Thirty-eight women killed by a man we—I?—have dubbed the Jackson killer, because of this calling card, a twenty dollar bill.

What no one knows is that inscribed on each twenty are the words, "thank you for your service."

Sick.

The only anomaly in the lineup of cases is still the murder of my old boss, John Booker.

My daughter's case, however, is absent, because, like I said, she doesn't exist.

Never existed.

See why I need to write things down? Because I sound a little crazy when I say it aloud.

"Rem. I thought I'd find you here."

The voice turns me and just like always I'm blown over by the sight of Eve walking onto a crime scene.

Her auburn hair is tied back, and she's wearing a pair of hiking boots, jeans and her CSI vest. And, she's just as beautiful as she was yesterday, or the day before, and twenty-three years ago when I kissed her on the steps of her home.

She's not mine. And she probably just rolled out of the bed she shares with Burke and I need to not let that find root in my brain if I hope to survive this world.

Time is cruel. Or maybe it's fate. I'm not sure, but frankly, Eve belongs to me. And I know that sounds rather Neanderthal, but that's just where I am right now.

I'm not sure why the idea of her, happy, with my best friend is worse than her divorcing me. I just can't believe she moved on after what we had. Or maybe we, like Ash, never existed because Eve looks at me with a friendly smile, nothing of a spark in her eyes, and my throat thickens.

I probably need more coffee.

No, I need to rewind time, find my life, and throw the watch into the Mississippi.

She is carrying a pair of gloves, but she doesn't do the heavy lifting anymore. Not as director of the Crime Lab.

She stands at the edge of the crime scene, stares at the body. "What do we know?"

This information is recent, handed to me by Zeke, my assistant. "Female, early twenties. From the marks at her neck, she was strangled. She's naked, but in her hand is—"

"A twenty dollar bill."

"Yeah."

"Is it marked?"

"Yes," I say and finish off my coffee.

"I hope we can get some DNA off her."

"Maybe, hopefully, she fought him," I say. "Look under her fingernails."

Eve gives me a look, but she's smiling. "We'll get him, Rem," she says. "By the way, why did you want me to pull the DNA off the Delany case?"

I stare at her, a coil tightening around my chest.

The Delany case?

Eve is snapping on her gloves. "Although, admittedly, I realized we didn't pull DNA the first time, so it's a good thing. I'm running the match through the CODIS database just to see if we get a hit on Fitzgerald."

Oh, right. Lauren Delany. The working girl killed outside Sonny's bar. She had a twenty in her pocket. Did I identify her as a Jackson murder? The first go-round, she was just an unlucky girl who'd been picked up by the wrong John.

Until now, that John was unnamed. But now, it's Leo Fitzgerald. The name is a recent acquisition to my memory, and it takes me just a moment to nail it. Leo Fitzgerald, the lead suspect in the Jackson murders. Former military, bomb-maker, and the man whose explosive ambush killed John Booker.

He's been in the wind for three years.

He's been the primary suspect since his DNA was found on his dead girlfriend, strangled, sexually assaulted and marked with the first of the Jackson bills. But that doesn't happen for two more years...or rather two years after Lauren Delany's case.

So what was I thinking?

Eve starts down the hill toward the activity, but I can't help myself. "Hey—how's your mom?"

She looked up at me. "She's good, Rem, thanks. But you just

two days ago at my Dad's memorial party." She is frowning.

The Danny Mulligan annual birthday party, the precinct-wide bash Bets has every year to celebrate her husband's life, even in death. So, I'm still invited to that? "Right. Yes, I just...I don't know." Two days ago, she lay bleeding in the sidewalk of Eve's childhood home. Catch up, Rem!

I need an assistant, one of those people who reminds me where I am, and why. But the right words form in my soul. "It's just been a long time since Danny's death, and I...you just don't get over losing someone you love, right?"

She gives me a smile, and it's sweet. "Sometimes, Rem, you remind me of a guy I used to know." She winks then and heads down the hill.

I can't breathe.

It was real. What we had. I saw it flash in her eyes—me, holding her in my arms, her smiling up at me a second before she kisses me.

It was real.

So, then...I think my heart is seizing. I need to sit down—

"Boss, we found some clothes." The words from Zeke shake me out of the spiral of despair and back to the investigation. "It looks like a t-shirt."

Zeke is young, maybe mid-twenties, with a man-bun and built like a guy who works out after hours. He sort of reminds me of me, back when I lived for this job. He's wearing a pair of dress pants, an untucked striped shirt, his sleeves rolled up, and purple evidence gloves. I really don't know much about him, but I like him. He's eager. And right now, he's the closest thing to a friend that I have, so I'm on him like Velcro.

Someone needs to point me in the right direction.

Zeke is directing one of the CSIs to take a picture of the

evidence he's pointing to.

I take a breath, give one glance back at Eve, walk over and crouch next to him as he holds up the underbrush around the shirt. "What, the killer tosses this away as he's fleeing?"

"Or maybe during the crime, and he didn't have the time to find it?"

Zeke holds the shirt up. "Pillsbury Diner. It's a place just across the street. Great burgers, live music."

I know the place, and the thought sends a strange heat through me. A conversation is forming in the back of my head. I can't quite make it out, but I will, give me, ahem, time. "Turn it over."

Again, I'm not sure why, but something in my gut just knows...

He turns the shirt over.

Aw...shoot.

A footprint.

I know I'm cheating, because I remember now a victim from a different time, laying in a hospital bed..."It happened so fast. I was coming out of work at Pillsbury's and I heard someone behind me. I started running, and he tackled me. He put his foot on my back and held me down...

I'm scrabbling for her name, but it's buried under layers of other memories.

"I wonder how she got here." Zeke says.

"He surprised her after work, as she was coming out into the parking lot." It's not a hunch—I'm remembering my bedside conversation with the victim. Her name...her name. It's lodged in the back of my brain.

But deep inside, I'm hoping that I'm wrong. That this woman is not the blonde I met in the hospital, the youngest daughter of a couple from the suburbs. "She probably ran, and he caught up to her." I gesture to the footprint. "He held her down."

"We'll get this tread into the database and see what we can find." Zeke says. He bags the evidence.

I walk over to the edge of the yellow tape, duck under it and hike down to the crime scene. Eve is looking at the body, the strangulation marks at her neck, the evidence of assault. She picks up her hands. "She chews her nails. Nothing to grab skin," she says. "And the DNA might be washed away. It looks like her body might have been pushed into the water, then pulled out."

Her hair is wet and muddy, her lower lip gray, split. My memory flashes, but it's too brief to capture.

"I found her purse!" Zeke shouts. He's standing near a park bench. Eve follows me as we hike up the hill. We wait for the photographer, then I glove up as Eve picks up the purse. It's small, the kind that a woman wears over her shoulder, to her hip. What does Eve call that—a clutch?

"It's a cross-body bag," Eve says as she opens it. "So it's funny that it would have fallen off. Unless she was surprised, and it fell off her shoulder as she ran." She pulls out a small wallet.

I hold my breath. Because I remember now. Hollie Larue. Age twenty-three. Pretty, despite the black eye, the split lip. Two younger siblings. Her voice is soft, shaky in my head. He told me not to scream…

Eve opens the wallet. Tucked inside is her driver's license.

I look away, to the river flowing downstream, past the stone bridge, into the horizon where time is beginning a new day.

And, as she reads the name, I brace myself.

"Her name is Hollie Larue."

Yep.

This death is on me.

MEET
DAVID JAMES WARREN

Susan May Warren is the USA Today bestselling, Christy and RITA award–winning author of more than eighty novels whose compelling plots and unforgettable characters have won acclaim with readers and reviewers alike. The mother of four grown children, and married to her real-life hero for over 30 years, she loves travelling and telling stories about life, adventure and faith.

For exciting updates on her new releases, previous books, and more, visit her website at www.susanmaywarren.com.

James L. Rubart is 28 years old, but lives trapped inside an older man's body. He's the best-selling, Christy Hall of Fame author of ten novels and loves to send readers on mind-bending journeys they'll remember months after they finish one of his stories. He's dad to the two most outstanding sons on the planet and lives with his amazing wife on a small lake in eastern Washington.

More at http://jameslrubart.com/

David Curtis Warren is making his literary debut in these novels, and he's never been more excited. He looks forward to creating more riveting stories with Susie and Jim, as well as on his own. He's grateful for his co-writers, family, and faith, buoying him during the pandemic of 2020-21, and this writing and publishing process.

9 781954 023031